Look what people are saying about Pam Mantovani's Cowboys of Burton Springs....

"I truly enjoyed everything about this book. Kendall and Logan were an awesome couple and their daughter Marissa is such a cutie . . . I read this story in one sitting—it had some drama, a great romance and a hot cowboy. What's not to love?

—*Therese Lopez, Amazon review of*
COWBOY ON HER DOORSTEP

It's been a while since I've read such a good book. Once I started, I couldn't stop reading. The author did a great job developing a relationship between Carter and Audra, and did not rush the relationship like many authors tend to do. Audra's past kept the plot interesting, but it wasn't overdone. This was an easy, feel-good read, and I would definitely recommend it to friends and family.

—*Amy Vida, Goodreads review of*
COWBOY ON HER PORCH

The characters have great backstories and depth of personalities, determination and strength. The storyline has its surprises and twists, as well as a few upheavals when the truth comes out and is misinterpreted. Loved the ending and the final truths that also come out. Well done.

—*Judy Gittleson Hendrickson, Goodreads review of*
COWBOY TO HER RESCUE

First and foremost, this is wonderful romance. The fact that it's set at Christmas time is an added bonus. Ms. Mantovani creates such warmth in her books and characters. Oh, and did I mention the setting and the update on people from previous stories? A perfect read for when you need something hopeful.

—*bestselling author Patricia Lewin on*
COWBOY UNDER THE MISTLETOE

Books by Pam Mantovani

COWBOYS OF BURTON SPRINGS

Cowboy On Her Doorstep

Cowboy On Her Porch

Cowboy To Her Rescue

Cowboy Under The Mistletoe

A Soldier at Heart

Cowboy in her Classroom

OTHER

The Christmas Baby Bargain

Christmas with a Cowboy

by

Pam Mantovani

Bell Bridge Books

This is a work of fiction. Names, characters, places and incidents are either the products of the author's imagination or are used fictitiously. Any resemblance to actual persons (living or dead), events or locations is entirely coincidental.

Bell Bridge Books
PO BOX 300921
Memphis, TN 38130
Print ISBN: 978-1-61026-227-9

Bell Bridge Books is an Imprint of BelleBooks, Inc.

Copyright © 2023 by Pam Mantovani

Published in the United States of America.

All rights reserved. No part of this book may be reproduced in any form or by any electronic or mechanical means, including information storage and retrieval systems, without permission in writing from the publisher, except by a reviewer, who may quote brief passages in a review.

We at BelleBooks enjoy hearing from readers.
Visit our websites
BelleBooks.com
BellBridgeBooks.com
ImaJinnBooks.com

10 9 8 7 6 5 4 3 2 1

Cover design: Debra Dixon
Interior design: Hank Smith
Photo/Art credits:
Cabin scene (manipulated) © Whitewizzard | Dreamstime.com

:Lwcc:01:

Dedication

For Dawson
whose innocent joy and pleasure
are the brightest lights at Christmas

Chapter One

AVERY MCCLAIN didn't cry when she signed the divorce papers. Tears, along with regrets, had disappeared as she'd fought her now ex-husband for what she wanted...what was rightfully hers.

Since he was a prominent attorney from a long line of prominent attorneys, it had not been an easy battle. Still, despite all his slick tactics, all his demands, all his legal maneuvers, she'd refused to bend.

When something mattered, when it was important, she fought to keep what had been given to her and her alone.

Timothy had argued harder and longer for the ownership of the cabin in Montana—the cabin she'd inherited from her uncle—than he did over signing away any and all claim to their daughter.

Walking out of the attorney's office, she smiled for the first time in months. A dark limo waited at the curb. The driver nodded as he opened the door, offering a hand to assist her inside the luxurious interior.

"You didn't have to do this."

"Of course, I did." Londyn Fitzgerald, her college roommate, wildly popular fantasy author, and Avery's only constant friend, waved a hand. "What's the point of being famous—and very, very rich—if I can't do something for my best friend?"

"He never even asked about her."

Londyn blew out a long breath as the driver pulled into traffic. "He never deserved sweet Brenna," she said, naming Avery's three-year-old daughter. "Or you."

"Well, now he doesn't have either one of us." She turned to peer through the smoke-tinted window. "I'm going to Montana."

"What? Why?"

"It'll be good for me and Brenna to have a fresh start."

"Come to New York."

"I love you for offering, but I feel like I owe it to Uncle Alex to use his cabin." She looked at Londyn. "Maybe I'm just being stubborn. Maybe I'm going simply because Timothy fought so hard to take it from me."

"Can't you just picture him, sitting there in one of his three-piece suits, in a hunting cabin?" Both women chuckled. "I'm sorry, Av," she said. "But what the hell did you ever see in him?"

"I was lonely. He saw that and used it for his own purposes." She frowned. "I won't let something like that happen again," she promised.

"And you think Montana is the place to start again?"

She shrugged. "I won't know if I don't go." A store sign caught her eye, and she pointed at it.

"The Christmas sales start earlier and earlier," Londyn commented.

"In Montana I can give Brenna a traditional Christmas with a real tree, snow, and the magic of Santa. And maybe it'll restore my faith in joy and goodness."

"Christmas shopping in New York could do that."

Avery laughed, wrapped an arm around her friend's shoulder. "I'll call you every week," she promised.

It took time. She packed up and shipped out the few items she wanted to keep, along with giving her new contractor time to complete necessary renovations to the cabin before they moved in. Londyn, as only an understanding and the best of friends would do, postponed returning to New York and completing the final installment of her fantasy series to provide moral support. The day Avery dropped off Londyn at the airport, she and Brenna began their cross-country trip.

She took her time driving. After all, a three-year-old could only stand sitting in a car seat for so long. She constantly talked to Brenna, warding off fatigue or restlessness until they stopped, either to run off energy or take in sights along the way.

They stayed at a quaint bed and breakfast in Tennessee, then toured the Kentucky Derby Museum. Brenna squealed with delight while Avery got nauseous at the top of the Arch in St.

Louis. Londyn laughed when Avery told her about the experience later that night during their weekly phone call. When road construction got in the way, she changed routes. Crossing into Montana, beneath an eye-searing blue sky where she spotted her first eagle, the vast landscape ranged from rugged mountains, already topped with snow, to dense evergreen forests and more lakes than she'd imagined.

Impatient to get to her new home, she skipped a drive through Yellowstone. "We'll come back," she promised Brenna, who played with the stuffed moose she'd become infatuated with at a truck stop.

She took time to stop in the town of Burton Springs and pick up some basic groceries before heading to the cabin. People nodded in that friendly smalltown way she'd come across once or twice during her travels. This time, however, it felt different. These would be her neighbors. Still, she rushed through her purchases and headed out, following the directions.

At the end of a long gravel road, she braked to a stop, shut down the engine and stared through the windshield, taking it all in. A hundred yards away was the cabin that held warm memories of an uncle who had welcomed her in the summers, given her the attention and love she'd so rarely known from her parents.

"Mama," Brenna cried from the back seat. "Out."

"Home," she corrected her daughter. "We're home."

"YOUR UNCLE WAS a heck of an outdoorsman, but a lousy housekeeper," Harley Barker said as he signed his name to the final document.

She'd arrived in Burton Springs two days ago and was now taking care of official business. Harley Barker, her uncle's attorney, was the first stop. "Whenever I visited Uncle Alex, I always felt like I was going on a treasure hunt," Avery recalled, thankful that the happy memories were starting to replace her guilt for having neglected him for so long. "I would find a bird's nest, an old arrowhead, a collection of elk antlers, a turtle shell he used as a bowl to hold rocks and nuts, and, once, a bear claw."

"The place is cleaned and updated for you now."

"I appreciate you taking care of everything," she said. The attorney had been helpful in so many ways since he'd informed her of her uncle's passing fourteen months earlier.

"I'm obliged to tell you I've been approached by someone to inquire if you might be interested in selling your property."

"No, I'm not."

"A hundred acres of land is a big responsibility for a young woman."

She smiled slightly. "You mean a young woman who's lived her entire life in a city in Georgia?"

He paused, glancing at the corner where Brenna talked toddler gibberish to a collection of stuffed animals. "I mean a single mother with a young daughter."

The reminder that she, and she alone, was responsible for her daughter's welfare could have depressed her if it hadn't been true since the day Brenna was born. Her ex-husband hadn't attempted to hide his disappointment at being told he had a daughter instead of a son. His loss, she thought now as she watched Brenna put the stuffed animals in a basket, then laugh when she tipped it over so they spilled out. His very great loss.

"I appreciate your concern, Mr. Barker."

"Harley," he reminded her. "It's a generous offer, one that could give you and your daughter a comfortable life."

"You know how hard I had to fight to keep this property." He nodded. "I have fond memories of the summers I spent here with Uncle Alex. I'm not going to dishonor his legacy by selling it off before the ink is dry on the deed."

"Do you have any idea what you're going to do with the land?"

"No, and to be honest, I'm not entirely sure I'll stay in Montana beyond Christmas." She pointed at the wall calendar a month shy of turning the page to November. "But I am looking forward to spending the holidays here."

"The town does it up right. There'll be plenty for you to do and see."

"I look forward to it."

Harley stood and offered his hand. "If you need anything, you know where to find me."

AVERY WAS USED to the stares. Although she had arrived seven weeks earlier, people in this small and close-knit community still looked at her as if she was a stranger rather than their newest neighbor. The bulk of those seven weeks she'd spent in the cabin, setting up house, acclimating herself and Brenna to their new surroundings. She'd had work deadlines to meet—she was just starting out as a graphic designer and knew that she had a reputation to keep up—and, she smiled a little, she'd also spent considerable time shopping for winter wardrobes.

Today, however, the stares were for a little girl who was fussy and tired. Avery knew she was blessed with a child who willingly went down for naps. The problem today was, with Thanksgiving two days away–she'd spotted some businesses already starting on their Christmas decorations—Avery had needed to run errands. And they'd taken longer than she'd anticipated. She wouldn't be preparing a traditional feast, or contacting a caterer to serve it for her ex-husband's family and associates, but she did want to make the day as special for her and Brenna as she could.

She glanced down into her cart. Most of the other shoppers had full ones, with the traditional turkey, stuffing, and other assorted items for big family gatherings. Tossed in with their discarded coats, her cart held a box of Breanna's preferred macaroni and cheese and a frozen lasagna for herself. Along with a nice bottle of wine.

"Brenna..." Avery rubbed a thumb on her daughter's palm, a gesture that, since birth, always calmed her. Her eyes, green like her father's, were heavy with fatigue and her full bottom lip, inherited from her mother, trembled against the urge to cry. "Okay, sweetie, we're going." It would mean a trip back to the store tomorrow, when it was likely to be a madhouse, but she would manage.

"Uh, oh. Looks like someone missed their nap."

Avery watched as a man leaned down to smile at Brenna. "I

know just how you feel, sweetheart. I get cranky myself if I don't get enough sleep."

Maybe it was a small town, but Avery didn't like the idea of a stranger being so close to her daughter. She unhooked the safety strap and lifted Brenna out of the seat . . . then gasped in surprise when Brenna flung herself into the man's arms.

"I'm sorry," Avery said, reaching for Brenna.

"No problem. Well," he said, smiling as he leaned back when Brenna reached out for the brim of his caramel-colored cowboy hat. "Maybe one. Sorry sweetheart, but no woman, no matter how cute, gets her hands on my hat." He removed it and tossed it into Avery's cart.

"She doesn't usually go to strangers," Avery said, nervously.

"Then let me introduce myself. I'm Judson, Judson Ford. I own the New Horizon Ranch."

"'Udson." Brenna said, earning a chuckle from him.

He pointed a finger at Avery. "And who's this lovely lady?"

"Mama."

Maybe because this man held her precious daughter so carefully, charming her by making funny faces and earning delighted giggles, Avery couldn't dismiss him outright, as she'd easily been able to do with every man who'd crossed her path in the past year. Still, she wouldn't let down her guard either.

Then, over her daughter's head, his eyes locked with hers. She felt a shock, an intense streak of fire, race down her spine. She had no idea what had caused it, had no idea why she'd felt it. All she knew was it wasn't entirely sexual in nature.

"I was sorry to hear about Alex Mitchell's death."

"Did you know him?"

"Our paths crossed from time to time, since his property borders mine." He paused. "Since it's yours now, that makes us neighbors."

"I'll keep that in mind in case I need a cup of sugar."

"That and a few other basics are about all I have in my kitchen."

Avery glanced down at her cart. "Maybe I should pick up some sugar to have on hand." She smiled at Brenna. "And for when I make Christmas c-o-o-k-i-e-s."

"That doesn't look like much of a Thanksgiving feast."

Heat rose on her cheeks. "Brenna's too young to have turkey, and it hardly seemed worth the effort to cook for one," Avery said.

"Can't blame you there."

Avery watched Judson's gaze move over her shoulder and warmth softened the dark color of his eyes.

"Audra," he said, pleasure evident in his voice.

Avery turned, surprised to find a woman pushing a cart. Inside it were two young boys, and another holding onto the cart handle. All three children were currently entertained with toy cars and action figures.

"Hello, Judson. I'm surprised to find you here."

"Audra Montgomery, this is Avery McClain. She's the new owner of the property next to mind."

"Oh, you're Alex Mitchell's niece. I didn't know him, but I've heard good things about him. Welcome to Burton Springs." Her features softened as she studied Brenna, who now had her head lowered to Judson's shoulder. "What a beautiful little girl you have." She sighed and stroked a hand over the small bump of her belly before reaching over to snag the car her three boys fought over. It took only a single look to stop the arguing. "I'll be outnumbered five to one come July."

"Carter's a lucky man," Judson said.

"No," Audra corrected him, smiling at her three boys. "I'm the lucky one."

"Audra and Carter got engaged on Thanksgiving," Judson said. "Since then, it's become a tradition for them to open their house to whoever wants to come."

"Please join us," Audra said. She nodded at Judson, a gesture of acceptance of what he'd been suggesting. "If you don't, I'll worry all day about you being alone."

"That's very kind of you, and I appreciate the invitation. Really. But Brenna and I will be fine." She hesitated. "We're used to being alone. And, as you can see, she likes her nap time."

"You talk funny."

"Bradley," Audra gasped with embarrassment.

"Well, she does. I didn't say she sounds bad." The boy standing at the handle hunched his shoulders. "It's kind of like music."

Avery leaned forward and tapped a fingertip to his nose, when what she really wanted to do was sweep him into her arms. "That, kind sir, is just about the nicest thing anyone's ever said to me."

"Hey," Judson protested. "Are you trying to steal away my reputation as the most eligible man in town?"

"No, sir. You're not 'pose to steal. Aunt Kendall will arrest you if you do."

"My sister-in-law," Audra said with a chuckle. "Is a deputy sheriff."

"Don't pay any attention to him. He's just jealous because you're so sweet," Avery said, grinning when the two other brothers made kissing noises. She straightened, looked at Audra, then gave in. If she wanted to become part of the community, she needed to participate. "What can I bring?"

"Nothing this year. It's your first time, and we always have plenty."

"Enough for me to take home a leftover dish?" Judson asked.

"Or two," Audra agreed. She brushed a hand over Bradley's hair.

"Really, I can't come empty-handed."

"A bottle of wine?" She looked at the boys. "Maybe something special for the kids?"

The boys piped up with their favorites and Audra gave Avery her address before she led the boys away to complete their shopping.

"I'll take her now," Avery said to Judson, holding out her arms, only to realize Brenna had fallen asleep.

"You don't want to wake her when she just fell asleep, do you?"

"And you want to hold her?"

"It's called being a good neighbor."

Avery gave in and selected two additional bottles of wine,

along with a bouquet of flowers for Audra, before picking out the drinks the boys had mentioned. Standing behind her as she paid for her purchases, Judson Ford kept up a conversation with the clerk, who bounced curious glances between him and Avery. When her transaction was complete, and her bags stored in the cart, she turned to Judson.

"I've got her."

"But it's cold outside," Avery protested, holding up Brenna's coat.

"I'll keep her warm."

Rather than make a scene in the front of the store, Avery said nothing and turned to push the cart toward her vehicle.

"This time next year, you won't even need a coat," Judson said beside her. She looked over to find him studying her.

"It's a long way from Georgia. Or is it Alabama? Tennessee, maybe? C'mon," he said when Avery looked at him. "Even before Bradley said anything, you knew we could all hear the magnolias in your voice. Or is it peaches?"

"Peaches," she confirmed as her lips twitched. "Atlanta to be specific." Using her key fob, she opened the rear hatch of her SUV and unlocked the doors before turning to him. She had the added feature of the engine starting, and therefore the heater going as well. "I'll get her strapped in the car seat if you don't mind putting the bags in the back."

She had a hand slipped between Brenna's body and his chest when she froze. It was, she realized, the first time she'd had to make this kind of transfer. Brenna's father had never held his daughter, not even as an infant.

"Are you okay?"

She nodded, completing the transfer. But she held Brenna close a moment, before moving to place her in the car seat. It was nice to have an extra pair of hands, someone to take care of the groceries while she settled Brenna. "Thank you," she said sincerely when he came to her door.

"What time should I pick you up on Thanksgiving?"

"I appreciate the offer, but I'd rather drive myself," she said, clicking her seatbelt in place. "I need to do some work that morning, and if I have my own car, I can leave if Brenna gets cranky."

He stepped back. "Okay. See you then."

Hours later, after dinner, bath, and cuddle time with Brenna before she fell asleep, Avery poured a glass of wine and thought back over the day. A part of her questioned how she'd allowed herself to be railroaded into spending Thanksgiving Day with strangers but another part of her had been warmed by the invitation. Besides, how could she deny the sweetness of having a small boy tell her that she sounded like music when she talked?

There'd been little sweet about Judson Ford. Oh, he'd been charming, but there'd also been a sharpness and intensity beneath that public layer. It reminded her, painfully, of why she was in Montana. She recalled Thomas' pursuit of her back when they'd been dating. At the time, it had been flattering to be the center of his attention.

Then again, Judson had made no effort to change her mind when she insisted on driving to the Montgomery ranch on Thanksgiving.

She roamed the central room, with an unobstructed view of the eating area and kitchen. The master bedroom and bath were on the other side of the cabin, with two remaining bedrooms, split by a bathroom, lining the rear of the house. A wide deck, now covered in a foot of snow, extended the front length of the house and would be a great place to sit outside in warmer months. Maybe she'd speak to Jessica Thorne, the woman who'd handled the renovations, about building a swing set for Brenna. And a rocker for herself.

It was a far different, more updated version of the house she'd stayed in while visiting her uncle. But the house had just been somewhere to be when they couldn't be outdoors. She'd had a different freedom here than at home. There had been so much to explore and discover. Uncle Alex had shown limitless patience as he taught her about the environment and respect for the wildlife.

He'd laughed with delight when she'd caught her first fish, had beamed with satisfaction when he taught her how to select and cut a thick branch to make into a hiking stick. She recalled the two of them sitting on the back porch, juice running down their chins from the first freshly picked tomato they'd grown together. He'd never been too busy to answer questions or explain something to her. He'd given her the attention her own parents had been too interested in their careers to offer.

She vowed Brenna would never doubt her mother's love.

Taking her wine with her, she went into the bedroom she'd set up as an office. She'd take her mind off disappointments, heartache, and the surprising attraction to Judson Ford by concentrating on work. If she succeeded in winning the graphic design contract for a national cookie company, it could make all the difference in the world for her and Brenna. Not only would it give her more financial security, but it would ensure she could keep working from home and always be available for Brenna.

Whether home ended up being here or somewhere else was a question to be answered later.

Chapter Two

"YOU'RE WORKING?" Avery wedged the phone between her chin and shoulder so she could pour coffee. She'd stayed up later finishing a project last night than she'd planned. Thankfully, Brenna was content playing with a doll at the moment. "Oh, Londyn. I hate knowing you're alone."

"No one is ever alone in New York. There are plenty of places I can go if I want. But, honestly, I'm fine by myself. I'm on a roll, and I really need to finish this last book."

"Last book? Then, you've decided for sure to end the series?"

"It's time, Avery. I . . ."

She set down her untasted coffee at the uncharacteristic hesitation in her friend's voice. "Londyn? What's wrong?"

"Nothing." The hurried reply didn't ease Avery's mind. "I'm just a little distracted with this last scene I wrote. It's not developing the way I imagined."

"Maybe you need a break. Why don't you come out here? You said the book isn't due until February. You could spend some time with me and Brenna. Stay for Christmas. It snowed, again last night."

"It snowed in New York, too."

"I bet my snow's prettier."

Her grin at Londyn's laugh faded as she glanced out the window. The pretty snow she'd mentioned completely covered the path from her house to the main road.

"I bet it is," Londyn said. "What I really want to know is . . . are the cowboys as rugged and good-looking as they are in books and movies?" This time, the hesitation was all Avery's. "Oh," Londyn cooed. "What aren't you telling me?"

"I met my neighbor, Judson Ford. Brenna took a liking to

him right away." She turned her back on her daughter. "Londyn, she hasn't once asked about Timothy."

"That's no surprise. She can't miss someone she's never known. She's got you, and you and I know that's more than either of us had. Now, tell me about this Judson."

"He's bald, twenty pounds overweight, chews tobacco, and is bow-legged from riding horses all day."

"He must have made an impression on someone other than Brenna if you're avoiding telling me about him."

"I'll let you know after today. I'm going to another ranch for Thanksgiving. Wish me luck."

"Oh honey, you've already got all the luck you need. Say hello to your cowboy for me."

Avery laughed and ended the call. If Londyn only knew . . .

A couple of hours later, as she settled Brenna down for an early nap, Avery heard a muffled engine. Taking her phone with her, she stepped onto the wide deck that fronted the house, surprised to see a tractor coming up her path, clearing snow.

With a gloved hand raised in greeting, the man driving the tractor continued working until he reached the edge of the deck and cut the engine. He looked to be early to mid-forties with the rugged good looks that Londyn had mentioned.

"Hello. Happy Thanksgiving." He flicked a finger at the brim of his hat. "I'm Daniel Gaines. My ranch, The Golden G, borders your property on the west side. I figured since you're new here, you wouldn't have a plow to clear your road."

"That's very nice of you, Mr. Gaines. I'm Avery McClain."

He nodded. "I heard you and your little girl came from Georgia." Now she nodded. "I've got a girl of my own." He chuckled. "She's sixteen and thinks she knows everything about everything."

"I remember thinking the same at that age."

"I tell myself that's the kind of attitude that will help get her what she wants when she's older. Plenty of people around her will tell you she inherited her stubbornness from me."

"I'm sure you and your wife are proud of her."

"Sadly, my wife's been gone for nearly eight years now."

"I'm sorry."

"You didn't know." He reached to turn on the engine, then paused. "My cook is known for her Thanksgiving feasts. I apologize for the last minute invitation, but you and your girl are welcome to join us."

"Thank you, but we already have plans. But I appreciate the offer."

His gaze narrowed, and Avery would have sworn she saw a lighting quick flash of temper before his features relaxed. "I'm glad to hear you won't be alone. I'll have to make sure I don't wait so late to invite you the next time."

"I'm really grateful to you for clearing the driveway for me. Uhm, if you'll tell me what you charge, I'll be happy to pay you."

"Nonsense. I killed two birds by coming out here and introducing myself while giving you a little help. That's what neighbors are for, right? You just be careful when you drive. Sometimes, there's ice under the snow."

Hours later, she took his advice to heart, slowly creeping along the cleared path. "There's no rush, right?" she asked Brenna, glancing in the rearview mirror.

"White, Mama."

"It sure is, baby."

Even when she reached the main road, she continued to drive carefully, following Audra's directions. "Okay," she said, taking a long breath as she parked alongside the other cars and trucks in front of a large two-story home. A wreath hung on the dark blue front door and she spotted Christmas lights already rimming the windows and porch railings. The door opened just as she lifted Brenna from her car seat. In a flannel shirt and jeans, Judson came down the steps.

"'Udson." Brenna held out her arms for him to take her.

"Hey, cutie." With an ease that had nothing to do with strength, he scooped Brenna high above his head, making her laugh. "I was just heading over to see if you needed a ride." He settled Brenna at his hip, then looked at Avery. "I wasn't sure if you'd had your road cleared or not."

"Daniel Gaines came by this morning and took care of it

for me. I offered to pay him, but he insisted he just wanted to help me out."

"I bet he did."

Avery shut the car door after she grabbed the bag of wine and the flowers. "Is there a problem?"

"Be careful around Daniel, Avery. He's not what he seems."

"He was perfectly polite. He even invited me to Thanksgiving dinner at his ranch."

Judson opened his mouth as if to comment, then closed it without saying anything.

She looked at him. "Why do I have the feeling there's more going on here than you being beat to the punch about clearing my driveway?"

"Daniel has a reputation for getting what he wants, using whatever means is necessary." Judson adjusted Brenna on his hip. "He wants your land."

"What makes you say that?"

"There's a large stream on your property."

"Yes, I know. Uncle Alex taught me to fish there."

"It'd be a good water source for Gaines's cattle, and the land would provide more pasture space."

"Harley did tell me he'd had a generous offer for the land."

"And?"

"I told him I could hardly think about selling when the ink on the deed wasn't even dry."

"And now that it has dried?"

"I'm not making any decisions until after the first of the year." She stroked a fingertip over Brenna's cheek. "I want to give her the kind of Christmas I never had."

"Then we should go inside," Judson suggested. "Can't get to Christmas without having Thanksgiving first." He held out his hand. "Call me if you ever need help, okay?"

Avery couldn't explain why her mouth suddenly went dry. Or why she couldn't seem to look away. She nodded.

"Cold, Mama."

"You're right, cutie," Judson said. "Let's get inside where it's warm. Besides—" He rubbed his nose against hers, eliciting a giggle. "That's where the food is."

Seeing its comfortable furnishings, and a clutter that clearly showed children lived here, Avery realized this was a home meant to be enjoyed and not simply admired. Already, a Christmas tree, strung with brightly colored lights but missing ornaments, stood in one corner. Children of assorted ages and genders ran around, chasing one another or playing together with the toys overflowing out of a wooden crate. Two girls, young teenagers, sat together, whispering and giggling. Avery watched her daughter walk over and immediately pick up a plastic horse.

Perhaps her attitude was skewed by past experiences during her marriage, but she had expected everyone to be polite but restrained. Instead, she found herself welcomed as if she was an old friend rather than a new resident. They asked questions of course, wanting to hear about her life and work in Atlanta. Several mentioned having known her uncle. There was the predicable division of women in the kitchen while the men kept an eye on the children. Avery was told, in no uncertain terms, that since this was her first Thanksgiving in Burton Springs, she was excused from any kitchen duty. Although, from what she could tell, Audra Montgomery had everything under control.

"You look like you could use this." Avery accepted the glass of white wine offered by a stunning woman in a snug blue dress. "And standing here with you keeps me from being expected to do anything domestic."

"Glad I could help."

"Rhonda," Audra admonished. "Be nice."

"I'm always nice," she said with a twinkle in her eyes. "Until it's more fun to be wicked."

Rhonda eyed her over the rim of her glass before her gaze slid to the side. Unable to resist, Avery looked . . .and felt her heart swell at the sight of Judson sitting cross-legged on the floor, Brenna cuddled on his lap while *helping* him play a card game with Audra's two youngest sons.

"You and your girl have excellent taste," Rhonda softly commented.

"She was taken with him from the start. He's so patient with her. I'm surprised he's not married with a family of his own."

It didn't surprise Avery that, even with all the noise coming from the other room, the sudden silence in the kitchen was like a roar.

"Okay, I've answered your questions about my divorce and why I moved here." With an openness she'd rarely offered, she added, "I don't let just anyone around my daughter, so tell me what you're trying not to say."

"Judson's a widower," answered Kathy Davis, a mother of two, who owned the feed store with her husband and had recently started a new business with Jessica Thorne, the contractor Avery had used to help fix up the cabin. "His wife was a marathon runner, training for the Olympics. She was out for a run when she was hit by a car."

Avery pressed a hand to her stomach. "That's awful."

"That's when Judson came back here and started his ranch." Kathy paused in her peeling of carrots. "Every one of us trusts him with our children. He'd never do anything to hurt your daughter."

It didn't surprised Avery that she and Judson ended up seated next to one another. The fact that the table was designed for ten but now sat fourteen, meant their arms and thighs brushed with each move. She quickly gave up trying to make space between them. After Carter offered some short, but lovely words about being thankful for family and friends, lively conversation competed with requests for the overflowing platters and bowls to be passed.

"You don't want pie?" Audra asked as three different choices were passed around the table.

"I'm not much for sweets, but I'd love some coffee."

"I'm not sure," said Kendall Montgomery, Audra's sister-in-law and a deputy sheriff. "I don't trust anyone who doesn't like sweets."

"I'll take her slice," Judson offered and, under the table, pressed his thigh against hers. "I'm practicing for Christmas cookies."

"I heard the mayor's setting up a cookie decorating contest

this year," Audra said. "Are you going to do the wagon rides around town again, Judson?"

"You don't think the mayor would let me get out of that, do you?"

"Wagon rides?" Avery asked.

"Yes, Judson gives horse-drawn rides every weekend during the holidays, starting this Saturday."

Avery tried to keep track of the conversation as everyone informed her of the town Christmas activities. Only the image of Judson driving a horse-drawn wagon kept running through her mind. She could easily picture him, his hat and coat covered in a dusting of snow, his profile lit from the lights hung around town, with people in the back singing along with the Christmas carols someone mentioned he played during the ride.

Thinking of how much she and Brenna would enjoy the ride, she glanced over at her daughter. Brenna's eyes were drooping.

"Looks like I need to get someone home," she said, picking up her cup to carry into the kitchen.

"No, Mama. Play, 'Udson."

"Didn't I hear you ask Audra about a tour of her studio?" he asked. "I'll keep an eye on her if you want to go out and take a look."

Given the way every woman in the room looked from him to her, Avery knew they'd be the topic of gossip the next day.

"I have a few Christmas ornaments left from Founders Day," Audra said. "You mentioned you needed some for your tree."

"I bought a half dozen," said Gabriella Ferguson, the town doctor.

There was no way out of it. Nodding to Judson, she followed Audra out of the room.

An hour later, Avery returned to the house with four ornaments for her tree, one to send to Londyn, a candle holder that held a six-inch-wide pillar and a cherry red bowl for her kitchen table. She found her daughter sound asleep in Judson's arms.

"I tried to keep her awake," he said. "But she just gave out on me."

"It's what she does."

"Can she teach ours?" asked Sydney Evans, referring to her five-month-old twin girls.

Judson stood. "I'll carry her out for you."

Audra draped a blanket over Brenna while Avery used her car fob to start the engine before she got her coat and said her good-byes. With the leftovers Audra insisted she take home stored in the trunk, and the back door closed, she turned . . .and bumped into Judson.

"Oh, sorry."

"No problem."

For one frantic heartbeat, as he leaned toward her, she thought he might kiss her. Whether or not she wanted him to became a moot point when he opened her door and stepped back.

"I'll follow you home."

"Oh, you don't—"

"You're not used to driving in this weather. Especially in the dark. I just want to make sure you don't run into any trouble." With a hand curled around her elbow, he guided her into the car, shut the door, then walked over to his truck.

She kept an eye on his headlights behind her all the way home. At the house, he left his truck running as he carried Brenna to the back door while Avery unlocked and stored her bags inside.

"Thank you," she whispered when he handed her the sleeping baby. "Drive careful."

"Happy Thanksgiving, Avery."

She stood in the back foyer, watching him through the window as he navigated his truck through the snow and drove away.

"He's a nice man," she whispered to Brenna as she carried her daughter into her bedroom. "Why does that make me nervous?"

JUDSON RAN A gentle hand over the muscular flank. "Oh,

yeah, you like that don't you?" he said, his voice soft. His hands continued to stroke, enjoying the softness as much as the strength.

"How about a ride, girl?" He moved his hand to the horse's nose and rubbed. "Feel like getting some fresh air, Nelly?" He moved over to scratch the neck of the German Shepherd he'd had since he started the ranch. "What do you say, Ginger? Want to have a run?"

"It's not speed or air you're after."

Judson didn't bother to look over his shoulder. He'd caught the odor that clung to his father's clothes before he'd spoken. Hodge Ford reeked of the two packs of cigarettes he smoked a day—the two packs a day he'd smoked for more than fifty years. Father and son had had a helluva argument over Judson's demand that Hodge not smoke in any of the buildings on the ranch. It was simply the latest of the many arguments father and son had fought over the years. While he'd been living in Chicago after college, Judson hadn't been able to prevent the housefire that had killed his mother. The fire that started because his father had dropped an unnoticed burning cigarette onto the throw rug under his recliner before heading out to his truck for a drive into town for supplies. It hadn't been intentional, but Judson wasn't going to take a chance of anything like that happening again.

Of course, accidents happened no matter what you did to prevent them. His wife hadn't planned on getting hit by a car during that last run after he'd stormed out of their apartment.

"Have you asked our new neighbor about selling you some of her land yet?" Hodge asked. "By the way, what do you want that land for anyway? Seems to me you've got plenty of it here."

Judson welcomed the talk of a potential for the future rather than the devastating losses of the past. Including the one he'd never told anyone about. "Jacob Reece over at the Double R asked me if I'd be interested in breeding with his thoroughbreds. If I do that, I'll need more pasture land."

"Don't see what's wrong with the horses you've got."

Ignoring his comment, Judson added, "The new owner fixed up the cabin. It could give you a better place to live than that shack at the back of the barn." He stood, spreading the saddle blanket over Nelly's back.

"Trying to get rid of me?"

"If I was, you wouldn't be working here."

That was another sore spot. Judson had built a ranch far and away better than anything his father had managed to scrape together. Shouldn't a father be proud of what his son had accomplished? Shouldn't a son want to help his father out of love rather than obligation? Too often it felt like the answer to both questions was no.

"I hear the new owner's a woman."

"Alex Mitchell's niece," Judson confirmed as he saddled the horse.

"I thought Harley told you she wasn't interested in selling?"

"I'm just being friendly and checking in on a new neighbor."

Hodge grunted as he followed Judson out of the barn. "You can fool yourself into thinking that, but I'm not falling for that line."

"Gaines went by there yesterday and plowed her driveway. He even invited her to dinner at his ranch."

It irritated the hell out of Judson to know the man had made an impression on Avery with his appearance. Not that Judson was above trying to do the same. After all he'd followed her into The Market a few days earlier hoping to find out what she was like.

"You think he's hoping to buy her land."

"He already made an offer."

Hodge swore, then stepped several steps away to light a cigarette. "You warn her about him?"

"I tried, but she strikes me as the kind who'd dig in her heels if I push too hard."

"Most women are," Hodge said as he blew out a stream of smoke. "I thought I'd work on that bit of fence that came down."

"You shouldn't be out in this cold. Stay inside and work on the tack. I noticed a couple of the bridles look like they could use an oiling." Judson swung onto the horse, scowling down as his father coughed even as he dragged in more smoke. "Those things are killing you."

"If not these, something else will," Hodge replied, as he had for as many years as Judson could recall.

"Maybe you should head into town and let Gabriella check you out," he suggested, naming the town doctor. "She asked about you at Thanksgiving yesterday."

Hodge's answer was to lift a foot so he could rub out the cigarette on his boot heel before heading back to the barn.

"Stubborn old fool," Judson muttered as he flicked the reins. Once he was out of sight, however, he drew out his cell phone.

"Doctor Ferguson," Gabriella answered.

"I've yet to figure out how you can sound so professional and yet sexy at the same time."

"Must be because I love my job. And my husband."

"It's almost your anniversary," Judson said, hearing the luxuriant sigh that conveyed her happiness.

"The first time Van and I were openly together was at Thanksgiving last year." Gabriella paused. "Is that something we'll be saying about you and Avery next year?"

Judson wasn't surprised by the question. He might be interested in Avery's land, but it was the woman herself who was on his mind. She intrigued him, and he couldn't resist finding out more about her. And that daughter of hers was a heartbreaker.

He thought again about Avery. Unlike the braid she'd worn when he'd met her at The Market, her golden-red hair had hung in a straight curtain to her shoulders yesterday. Her laughter had been light and quick, if infrequent, accenting the fullness of her lips. The brown of her sweater had brought out the gold in her amber eyes, and it had hugged her small breasts the way he fantasized about doing.

"Doc, I didn't call to discuss my pretty new neighbor."

"But you agree she's attractive?"

Judson ground his teeth. "Yes."

"And her little girl seemed quite taken with you."

It took no effort to relax and recall the pleasure of holding Brenna, the little girl who had curls her mother didn't have, and green eyes. And that cute way she had of saying his name and holding out her arms to him? Well, he knew when he was beaten. When she climbed onto his lap later in the day and had fallen asleep, he'd experienced a piercing pain for the loss of the child his wife had taken measures not to have.

He reined his horse to a halt at the crest of a small hill. In the valley below, he scanned the flat land. While now covered in snow, apart from the cleared ribbon of roadway, he visualized horses grazing in the summer, drinking from the stream he knew ran parallel to her western boundary. He took in the house, a tidy little A-frame. It would be a bonus and a definite step up from where his father lived now. If he could convince the stubborn man to move.

But what he really wanted was the land. Shifting in the saddle, he flicked the reins and started the slow approach toward the house.

Continuing his phone call, he said, "The reason I called is because my father was hacking up another lung when I left. Nothing new there, I know," he said to Gabriella. "But it worried me. I know you're going to the wedding out at the Double Diamond Ranch, but, maybe on your way home, would you have time to stop by and give him a quick look?"

Once he finished up with Gabriella, who promised to let him know about her visit with his father, he approached the house. Windows gleamed in the weak sunlight, and a thick layer of snow covered the deck. Ginger, true to form, sniffed around the edges of the deck and the few bushes that poked through the snow. She scampered back when he swung off the horse.

"Yeah, I know." He rubbed her. "It's pretty as a picture. Now—" he said when he heard a door open. "You be on your best behavior, okay."

Keeping a hand on Ginger's neck, and his fingers wrapped around Nelly's reins, he waited while Avery, carrying Brenna, took a cautious step onto the deck.

"'Udson."

"Hello there, cutie," he answered as Avery kept her from lunging toward him. For one brief instant, he wasn't sure if he was talking to the mother or the daughter. "I was out for a ride and thought I'd stop by to say hello."

"Horsie. Doggie."

He nodded to the horse. "This here is Nelly." He leaned over to rub the dog. "And this is Ginger." Straightening, he nodded toward the chimney. "I thought I'd check to see if you had enough firewood. It's always a good idea to keep some on hand in case the power goes out."

"I have gas logs."

"Makes life easier. I have them myself as a matter of fact." He stroked a hand down Nelly's neck, as he scanned the surroundings. "Sure is a pretty piece of property you have here. I can't blame Gaines from hoping you'll sell." He looked back at her. "In the interest of full disclosure, I'll tell you I'd like to have it myself."

"Then I'll say to you what I told him. I'm not making any decisions until after the first of the year. I want Brenna and I to have Christmas here."

"Fair enough."

"What are you doing?" Avery demanded when he let the reins drop, knowing Nelly wouldn't stray, and reached for the snow shovel propped against a corner of the house.

"Thought I'd shovel off your deck. And the walk to your car."

"Does this have anything to do with Daniel coming by yesterday and clearing the driveway."

"It's not a competition." He pointed at Brenna, who'd gone wide-eyed at the brusque tone of his voice. "I don't like leaving here thinking you might take a spill while you're carrying her out to the car." He watched Avery wrestle with his words. "Tell you what? I'll trade shoveling snow for a cup of hot coffee before I head back to my ranch." With a wary nod, she turned and went back into the house.

Judson scooped up the first shovelful of snow, pitching it

off to one side. Ginger, as she often did, chased after the snow he heaved, her yips and barks echoing in the stillness. Overhead, he heard the scream of an eagle and at one point, he caught the tail of a deer running through the woods. His breath misted in the air while sweat gathered at the small of his back. Once he paused long enough to mold and wing a snowball, grinning as Ginger dashed after it.

When he turned back to shovel more, he caught sight of Brenna, her nose pressed against the window, watching him. Unable to resist, he flicked a shovelful of snow in her direction, startling her into taking a step back, then laughing. With a wave of his hand, he turned back to his task.

He usually enjoyed this kind of work, the kind that kept the body toned and the mind free to go where it wanted. Today, however, his thoughts circled around the cautious woman inside the house. Twice, he'd caught her watching him through the tall window overlooking the deck. Only, unlike Brenna, she wasn't laughing.

He didn't take Avery's hesitation about his showing up personally. Especially after his confession that he was interested in her property. He wondered if she was naturally cautious or if it was the result of her divorce. After all, he was less willing to trust a woman after learning of his wife's betrayal.

Once he had the deck and walkway cleared, he located the outdoor water faucet and, stretching out his arm, let Ginger and Nelly drink their fill from the end of the hose. From the saddlebag, he pulled out and offered a dog biscuit and two sugar cubes. He'd just finished rolling up the hose when he heard the door open.

"Coffee's on." He looked over his shoulder. Avery stood in the doorway, her gaze focused on Nelly. "Are your horse and dog going to be okay out here?"

"They'll be fine."

She smiled a little. "Brenna's asking if she can pet them."

"How about this." He stepped close to the door and stomped his feet to get the snow off his boots. "You can bundle her up before I leave, and I'll bring her out to meet them. They're both gentle," he added at her hesitation. "You don't have to worry."

"Yes, I do." She opened the door wider. "Come inside."

Chapter Three

AVERY TRIED NOT to be suspicious of him. After all, the man had admitted he wanted her land. And while he claimed he wasn't here to convince her to sell—and she had no intention of doing so anytime soon—she wouldn't lower her guard and trust him.

Even if his motives weren't so innocent, at least she had her deck and walkway cleared. For the time being.

While she'd watched him from inside the warmth of her new home, she'd admired the way he moved, the strength in his arms as he scooped and pitched the snow. Then there had been the foolishness she'd observed as he played with his dog. And, as he often had in such a short time, with Brenna.

In the alcove off the back door, he slipped off his boots and shrugged out of his coat, hanging it and his hat on an empty hook of the wall that had once been an enclosed closet. Now there was a bench below, with baskets for assorted items.

"Doggie?" Brenna asked, raising her hands so Judson would lift her. Before Avery could say he shouldn't feel obligated, he had her in his arms.

"The doggie's outside, having a snack."

"Snack."

Avery's heart went to mush when Brenna turned hopeful eyes to her. Then, damn it, Judson turned an equally appealing look toward her. "I could go for a snack."

"A banana?"

Brenna shook her head. "Cookies."

"There's a girl after my own heart." Judson rubbed his nose against hers before looking back at Avery. "Cookies?" he asked with an innocence that was at odds with his dark masculine good looks.

"Cookies," Avery relented. A little bit of sugar seemed the lesser of two evils compared to the temptation Judson presented.

"Cozy," Judson commented as he followed her into the kitchen, still holding Brenna.

"It's roughly a quarter of the size of the kitchen I left behind in Atlanta," she said, glancing around the room.

The cabinets, and appliances were the pale gray of a morning mist. She'd added a pop of color by changing out the cheap metal handles on the cabinets with navy blue knobs. Nostalgia had tempted her to keep the Formica countertops but Jessica had convinced her to update it with white quartz. The floors were the same wide-plank wood that ran throughout the house.

"This one suits me better," she added. "You can put Brenna in her booster seat."

"I grew up in a two-bedroom cabin, about forty miles from here. It was even smaller than this one."

"Trust me, when I spent time with Uncle Alex, the cabin didn't look like this."

"I'm very sorry about your loss. He was an interesting man. Everyone liked him." Judson secured Brenna in the booster and made himself at home by opening the refrigerator and pulling out a carton of milk. "Cup?" he asked. She held out a sippy cup she pulled down from the cabinet.

"Uncle Alex was wonderful to me whenever I visited. I hope he'd be happy with the changes I've made."

"It's interesting that our paths never crossed whenever you were here in summer."

Brenna kicked her feet against the chair as she greedily took a long drink, only to drop it on the table when Avery offered a cookie. "Cookie," she cried when Avery held it back out of reach, lifting a brow at her daughter.

Brenna straightened the cup. "Pease."

Judson chuckled as he opened cabinet doors until he found two mugs. "I remember my mama having that knack. She wouldn't say a word but I'd know exactly what she meant."

"I have to work at it," Avery admitted. "It would be so easy to spoil her." She stroked Brenna's hair, watching as the child eagerly munched on the cookie. "To give her everything she doesn't have."

He abandoned the coffee and walked over to where she stood against the counter. "From what I can see, she's not missing a thing." He lifted a hand as if to touch her hair, only to drop it back to the countertop. "But it looks to me like you're the one missing something."

Her pulse kicked into high gear. It had been so long since she'd considered her needs that for a moment, her mind went blank. She'd always been careful where men were concerned. She'd dated in high school, but nothing serious. In college, she'd indulged in two affairs, neither of which held the power to change her mind about moving to New York and pursuing her graphic design career.

During the years she'd taken care of her father, she'd hardly had time to focus on her career, let alone have a personal life. Then, she'd met Thomas.

In hindsight, she could admit she'd been lonely, and very vulnerable after her father's death. The freedom from responsibility she'd so craved hadn't filled her the way she'd imagined it would. Instead, she'd stayed in Atlanta, in her parents' house, and continued to work as a free-lance graphic designer. Gone were her dreams of a having a high-powered career in New York. Instead, she found she enjoyed the quiet lure of working for herself, at her own pace, choosing her clients.

She looked at Brenna. "I've got everything I need."

"No, you don't."

Her gaze snapped to his, and she felt a punch of interest when he smiled. "You don't have coffee or a cookie."

"Oh, well, I'll take the coffee." Her heart drumming, she shifted to fill the two mugs. "But, if you remember, I shocked everyone yesterday when I announced I'm not much for sweets." She watched, amused when he added a generous serving of milk to his before he took three cookies from the glass jar nestled in the corner. "Now, if there was a bag of chips or pretzels between us, I'd fight you for them. Although after yesterday, I can't imagine wanting to eat anything for a week or so."

He nudged her with his shoulder. "Aren't you glad Audra convinced you to come?"

"It was a lovely day," she said, thinking back to her initial shyness at arriving at the Montgomery ranch. "I stayed longer than I'd planned, but they made me feel so included, I couldn't bring myself to leave."

"You sound surprised."

"No. Sad."

"Because you missed your family? Your friends?"

"I don't have friends or family. My parents are both gone. Uncle Alex was all I had left. My ex-husband has already remarried . . . to the mistress who gave him the son I didn't."

Avery wished she had a cookie to stuff in her mouth. Why had she confessed that to a near stranger? On the other hand, she'd learned of the loss of his wife.

"So, no, I missed no one." She concentrated on not looking at him, wondering if he'd thought of his wife yesterday. "Somehow that seems sadder than if there'd been a hole in my life that I used your friends to fill."

"They're your friends now too."

"Doggie."

Avery smiled at her daughter's demand. "Don't ever promise her something unless you're sure you'll follow through. She forgets nothing," she told Judson, turning to wet a paper towel so she could clean the mushed cookie off Brenna's cheeks and hands.

He reached for her, the cool, wet paper caught between their hands, a direct contrast to the heat in his gaze.

"I never make a promise I don't mean to keep," he said. She couldn't decide if he was simply making a point about friendship. Or warning her that he wasn't giving up on convincing her to sell. Either way, she knew better than to put any faith in his statement.

"Doggie."

She watched as everything about him relaxed. There was no denying he had a soft spot for Brenna. In quick fashion, he had

Brenna's hands and mouth cleaned up, then lifted her out of the chair.

"Would you mind if I brought Ginger inside?" he asked, tilting his head toward the back door. "She's housebroken and well-behaved."

"That's fine."

With the same ease he'd shown before, he carried Brenna down the hall. In no time, Avery heard the excited squeal, followed by Judson's low tone, she assumed both cautioning Brenna and soothing Ginger. Avery pressed a hand to her heart when a smiling Brenna returned to the kitchen, walking beside the dog that nearly came to her shoulder.

When the dog moved to block Brenna, Avery stepped forward, only to draw up short when Ginger lowered to her haunches and tilted her head at Avery. It was as if she was saying *I'll protect her.* She relaxed further when Brenna wrapped her arm around the thick coat and buried her face in the dog's neck.

"Doggie, Mama."

"I see."

Just as she could see Brenna had fallen in love. Avery lifted her gaze to Judson. "What do I do now?" she asked.

"Hope Santa has an extra puppy on his sled?"

"There's not much I wasn't prepared to give her this Christmas. But a puppy? I don't know."

"Never had one?"

"No. My parents were always at work or at some function or professional appearance. My ex, well, let's just say he wasn't the kind to tolerate having dog hair on his clothes."

Judson glanced down at how Ginger accepted Brenna crawling over her. He looked back at Avery with a smile. "You're always welcome to stop by my ranch for a visit whenever you like."

"Careful. You could be opening yourself to daily visits."

"No problem."

There would be if he continued looking at her the way he was now. She'd never had a man look at her with the intense interest she saw in his gaze now. A part of her—the part that had been damaged by learning of her ex-husband's multiple affairs—was flattered that he found her attractive. However, for that very reason, she needed to be cautious.

"Yes, well, we should let you get on with your day." She glanced over, her heart melting when she discovered Brenna half-asleep, snuggled next to Ginger. "And I think someone's ready for a nap," she whispered.

"May I?" he asked, stepping forward and crouching.

His fondness for her daughter no longer surprised her. Telling herself she was simply saving herself the exertion of lifting her daughter's sleepy weight, she nodded. His arms went under Brenna's body, lifting her in his arms. For an instant, he paused, looking down at her little girl's face with enough warmth to make Avery wish they'd met under different circumstances.

"This way," she said, clearing her throat. Because of the narrow hallway, he and the dog followed behind her to her daughter's room. When she used to visit her uncle, this room had been a hideous brown. One of the first things she'd done was have the walls painted a soft lavender—the perfect color to ensure a restful sleep for the most important person in her world. She stepped aside so Judson could place Brenna on her bed. Ginger sniffed at the dresser before moving over to the small table and chairs where Brenna liked to color before she checked out the cradle that held two abandoned dolls.

"Nice room," he said, stepping back so Avery could remove Brenna's shoes and cover her with a light blanket. Then she leaned down to brush a kiss over Brenna's cheek.

"Sweet dreams, baby."

She straightened, turned, intending to turn on the baby monitor, only to stumble over Ginger. Before she could fall, Judson caught her.

"Thanks."

He smiled. "My pleasure."

"Is she okay?" she asked, intending to look down at the dog, but unable to turn away from Judson.

"She is." His gaze lowered to take her in. Avery became very aware that their thighs were pressed together. And it wasn't because of a crowded table. Instead, she was sharply reminded of the pleasure at being held in a man's arms. Then, the sound of a phone ringing broke the silence and he abruptly released her and stepped back. He drew his cell out of his back pocket and glanced at the screen.

"Hello Gabriella." Judson grinned. "I bet he wasn't." He nodded as he remained silent, squatting down to run a soothing hand over Ginger's fur. "I appreciate it. I will." He rose, nodding again. Cocking his head, he gestured to Avery that they should head back to the kitchen as he continued the phone conversation. "How was the wedding?"

Avery could hear the feminine voice on the other line, but not the words. Avery went to the counter and turned on the monitor, then wet another paper towel and wiped down the table.

"I bet," Judson repeated and this time his voice was more indulgent. "Thanks again, Doc. Tell Van hello." Ending the call, he shoved the phone in his back pocket. "Sorry for the interruption." He paused. "My father's a heavy smoker and he was coughing a lot before I left today. I asked Gabriella to stop by and check on him."

"Is he going to be okay?"

"He's too damn onery to be anything else. Sorry." He dragged his hands through his hair, stopping her from asking more. "We don't exactly see eye-to-eye."

"And yet you had someone check on him." Avery emptied the cold coffee and refilled the mugs with fresh. "Does he live with you?"

"In a manner of speaking." He accepted the offered mug and followed her to the round table with four navy and white placemats. The red bowl she'd bought at Audra's held the banana Brenna had rejected. To Avery's surprise, Ginger padded over and settled at her feet. "I won't let him live in the house because of his smoking, so he lives in a place hardly more than a shack at the back of the barn."

"I spent three years after college caring for my father. He had a stroke while driving home after my college graduation. My mother died instantly in the crash." She sipped her coffee. "Needless to say, my plans drastically changed. I'd planned to move to New York and take the position I'd been offered at a prestigious marketing firm. Instead, I stayed in Atlanta and slowly built my graphic design business."

"Did you resent the choice being taken away from you?"

"But it wasn't. I could have hired help for my father. He and my mother had substantial investments that would have provided ample care. But I made the choice to stay. And that choice led to others, some that weren't so well thought-out." She glanced over at the monitor. "I've had the unique experience of caring for someone I love at the end and at the beginning of life." She looked back at Judson. "Sorry, didn't mean to get so philosophical."

"We all go through times when we look over our choices." He hooked an arm over the back of his chair. "I've done my share of pondering since I came back to Burton Springs."

"I have to confess, I was told yesterday about your wife's death. I'm sorry."

As if sensing his disquiet, Ginger rose from where she'd settled at Avery's feet to place her head on Judson's thigh. He stroked her, his hand slow and gentle.

"At first, they thought the driver had run a red light. But an investigation proved the light was faulty and that was the reason he'd thought he had the right of way. There was a settlement with the city so I came back here and built my ranch." He looked at her, his fingers still stroking Ginger's head. "One of the things I think about from time to time is how her death gave me what I wanted all along."

"And now you want my land too?"

"A rancher always wants more land."

"Why?"

"There's a ranch over in the next county, The Double R. It's been a family enterprise for generations, and they've raised some of the finest thoroughbreds in this area. They're looking for new stock to breed with theirs and asked me if I was interested."

"Obviously, you are."

He nodded and took a sip of his coffee. "It would be a big boost to my breeding operation. The problem is, my barn is too small to accommodate additional horses."

"So, my land would give you room to do what? Build another barn?"

"It would provide additional grazing land." He leaned forward. "I understand you have a sentimental attachment to this place, Avery. But, living this far from town, all by yourself... It's not going to be easy."

"It's not like I'll be growing crops or anything that will require supervision."

"What are you going to do with it?"

"I haven't decided yet." She smiled. "I'm looking forward to Christmas too much to worry about something I can't change in the next month."

"You wouldn't have to worry at all if you sold now."

"Judson, I should warn you up front, I'm not easily swayed once I have my mind set." She stood. "I'm sure you need to get back to your ranch."

"Here's your hat, there's the door?"

"Your hat is by the door."

She liked, a little too much, the humor that brought a bright light to his hazel eyes. She lowered a hand to stroke Ginger's head.

"I promised your little girl she could pet the horse."

"She'll be down for her nap for another hour."

"And you don't want me hanging around."

The problem was, she thought she would enjoy that too much. "It's just that I usually use nap time, or after she goes to sleep at night, to catch up on my work."

"Then I won't keep you." At the alcove of the back door, he sat and put on his boots. "I don't like breaking promises," he said, standing and shrugging into his coat. "Why don't you bring Brenna out to the ranch in a day or so and I'll show her more than one horse."

She glanced out the window of the back door. The horse he'd left there seemed harmless enough as it stood still beneath the overhang of the shed. Then she compared the animal's size to her tiny daughter's.

"She won't be in any danger," he said, as if reading her thoughts. "I promise."

She was all too aware that people could lie when they made promises. Just as she knew some people could look you in the eye with all apparent sincerity while they lied to your face. The fact that she hardly knew Judson Ford was the perfect reason why she shouldn't believe his words. And yet she did.

"Alright," she agreed.

"Where's your phone?" he asked, his voice too low and soft for such a common question.

"Uhm. In the kitchen."

"Go get it." He smiled when she hesitated. "I'll give you my number so you can let me know when you're coming."

"Oh, right."

Flustered, she spun on her heel and practically jogged to the kitchen. "Here," she said, offering it when she returned. God, he looked so damned appealing in that cowboy hat pulled low over his forehead and a fleece-lined coat covering his broad shoulders.

His gloveless fingers tapped buttons as he added his contact information, then pushed the call button. His phone chimed in his pocket, but he looked back at her rather than at his screen.

"Now, I've got your number too." He flicked the brim of his hat with a finger. "I look forward to seeing you again, Avery."

She let out a long slow breath when he finally stepped outside. Through the door window, she watched him settle in his saddle, give the horse a gentle stroke before he glanced back and nodded at her. He made a picture, with the dog by his side, as he and the horse moved as one.

The image remained imprinted in her mind as he disappeared over the horizon. She shook her head. How she was supposed to get any work done now?

JUDSON STOOD at the kitchen sink, watching the sunset sky bleed with reds, blues and purple, eating the sandwich that served as his supper. He really needed to get better about taking stuff out of the freezer and cooking. Maybe he should look into those meal boxes you could order, the ones that come with all the ingredients and instructions.

But what he was really doing was avoiding the issue that had plagued him all afternoon.

When he'd heard Alex Mitchell had willed his property to a niece in Atlanta, he figured she'd snap up his generous offer. Only he hadn't expected that niece to be so determined to forge a new beginning. And he couldn't even be angry about it. He appreciated and admired her resolve, understood she wanted to put the past behind her. After all, he'd done much the same when he returned to Burton Springs and built this house and ranch.

It was a damn shame their mutual desire was at cross-purposes.

He blew out a breath. When was the last time he'd felt so attracted to a woman? Physical desire, sure, that was easy. But there was more to Avery McClain than a pretty face and sexy body.

By her own admission, she'd set aside the chance of having a high-powered career to care for her father. Because he'd researched her, he knew she was smart and talented enough to have established a modestly successfully career as a graphic designer. From Harley, he knew she'd blocked her ex-husband's every attempt to take the land her uncle had left her . . .though that same ex had given her sole custody of their child without a fight.

Was it any wonder she refused to discuss any possibility of him buying her place?

He could offer to lease. Or maybe buy a portion of the land. The problem was, he wanted it all. And he was beginning to like Avery too much to pressure her into selling.

Washing down the last bit of his ham sandwich, Judson took a long pull of his warming beer. Because he was in the habit, although he'd never admit it, his gaze tracked over to the shack where his father lived. The small red dot of a lit cigarette glowed in the dark outside the front door.

"Damn fool. He's not going to be happy until he kills himself, too."

After letting Ginger out for her nightly round, Judson walked through the house. It was too large for a single man. He'd known that when he built it. Despite his crushing disappointment at learning his wife had ended any chance of her getting pregnant, he still had dreams of this house one day being filled with baby cries and the sound of footsteps running up and down the stairs.

Tonight, though, he climbed them in silence, with only the company of the dog beside him. And thought of a woman whose voice sounded like music.

Chapter Four

THE NEXT MORNING, as the sun rose over the horizon, Judson again stood at the window over the kitchen sink. He hadn't slept well and blamed last night's thoughts as the cause. His attention shifted when a light in the barn winked on. His father was an early riser, the one trait they shared.

"Morning nicotine craving," Judson murmured, then glanced down when his phone vibrated on the countertop.

"Good morning, Avery." He hadn't expected her to call so soon after his visit yesterday.

"While I appreciate you shoveling my deck yesterday..." she said abruptly—he could hear a hint of temper underscoring those fluid Southern tones—"I would have appreciated it more if you had turned the outside faucet all the way off after you watered your dog and horse." She drew in a breath that told him she wasn't finished. "Thank goodness I wasn't holding Brenna when I slipped on the ice this morning."

"Are you hurt?"

"No, I managed to hold my balance. Barely." She drew in another breath, one that wasn't as successful in calming her tone of voice. "If you think this kind of trick will convince me to sell, you're sadly mistaken."

"Now, wait a minute." He shifted the phone from his ear when he realized she'd had the last word and had hung up on him.

"Ginger," he called out after he'd put on his boots and a coat. Since he'd already figured out Avery would do just about anything for Brenna, the dog would distract some of her anger. And give him a chance to take a closer look.

It took effort and focus not to drive faster than was smart. He wouldn't be any help if he skidded off the road and into an embankment. He let out a long breath of relief when he parked behind her SUV.

He'd no sooner gotten out of his truck, with Ginger close behind, when the back door opened and there she stood, holding Brenna.

"I don't appreciate being accused of something I didn't do," he said.

"Who else would have done it? I certainly didn't touch the faucet."

That's what worried him. A layer of ice ran the length of the ground from the back door to where the faucet and hose lay. His heart was thundering in his chest; it had been, he admitted, since her phone call. He didn't want to think what might have happened if she'd taken a spill when she'd been carrying Brenna. They could have been out in this weather for hours.

"I tried to warn you that Daniel Gaines would do whatever he thought was necessary to convince you to sell your land to him."

"You're implying he did this?"

"No, he's too smart to do the work himself."

"Doggie," Brenna squealed, stretching out one arm.

"Go back inside," he told Avery. "Ginger." When he flicked a hand toward the house, the dog obediently went inside. Avery set Brenna down to chase after her.

"You didn't do this," she said, her voice hollow as he used the shovel edge to break up the ice.

He stopped to stare at her. "We don't know each other but, as much as I want your land, I'd never do anything to put you and Brenna in danger in order to have it."

"I'm sorry. I didn't know what else to think."

He nodded. "Go back inside," he repeated. He noticed she wore only a long-sleeve T-shirt with jeans, one that clung to her breasts in an alluring way. "Before you catch cold."

After a short hesitation, helped along by Brenna's squeal, she went inside. Judson returned to breaking and removing the ice. When he uncovered a discarded matchbook, he squatted down. Wet from being buried in ice but new enough that he knew it hadn't been discarded long ago, he stared at the emblem on the cover.

"The Golden G," he swore.

Throughout his first two years of building the ranch and establishing his business, Daniel had tried to talk Judson into selling. There had been a suspicious fire along the northern boundary where he was in the process of establishing a hay field. A couple of feed deliveries were either mixed up or delayed and several lengths of fencing had been damaged.

Just as he'd had no proof that Daniel had been involved in those incidents, he had none now that Daniel had orchestrated this water leak. But he knew the man could be ruthless when it came to getting what he wanted. There'd been at least four other ranch owners who'd finally succumbed to pressure and clashes before selling their property to Daniel, giving him the largest ranch in the county.

Avery opened the door as he approached. "I've got fresh coffee."

"Appreciate it." He closed the door, removed his hat, and sat to tug off his boots. "I found a matchbook with the logo of The Golden G."

"Should I call the Sheriff?"

"Not much he can do. Daniel will claim the matchbook has been here since before you moved in." Judson stood. "I know you met him and think he's charming. But I'm telling you he's as slick as that ice you found this morning. You don't want to let down your guard where he's concerned."

"You're trying to frighten me."

"No. I'm asking you to trust me and tell me if you have any other incidents around here."

"Are we in danger?"

Brenna toddled into the narrow hallway and Judson, without thought, swung her up into his arms. "Not if I can help it."

"'Udson, hi."

Smiling at the way she mangled his name, he nuzzled his nose against her cheek.

"Cold, Mama," she giggled.

"All warm now." With a wink for Brenna, he looked at Avery. Her features were soft, her eyes dreamy. "But I'll still take that coffee," he said.

"I'm sorry if my call took you from something important at your ranch."

"This time of year, most of the work is maintenance and preparation for spring. Hmm, hot and strong," he said after the first sip of coffee, still looking at her. "Just the way I like things."

"You're trying to distract me," she said, a pretty shade of pink color rising on her cheek.

"I can think of several, more satisfying ways to distract you."

"I have more than my share of distractions, thank you. Brenna's still adjusting to our new home and routine, so she's been irritable, demanding most of my attention when she's awake." she explained. "When she finally settles for the night, I have work to catch up on, hoping to get ahead of deadlines and projects so I can enjoy Christmas."

"Graphic design, right?"

When she nodded, Judson didn't hesitate. She'd just given him the perfect way of keeping a close eye on her.

"Do you have time to set-up a website and logo for my ranch? Whenever it's convenient for you," he blurted. "If you and Brenna come out to the ranch, I can give you an idea of what I'm doing, what might show best on a website." He grinned down at the little girl. "You haven't dropped by like you said you would so I can show Brenna the. . ."

"Don't say it," Avery interrupted, holding up a hand. "Or she'll be asking the rest of the day."

He leaned forward, barely resisting the temptation to kiss her. "Then say you'll consider my proposal."

"Blackmail?" she asked.

"Why don't we just agree that you'll come out to the ranch and look around?"

"When?"

"Whenever you want. My schedule's more flexible than yours."

He signaled Ginger, who rose to her feet. Brenna got up too, and started to run towards him. "Doggie stay," she said, wobbling enough that both Avery and Judson reached out to stabilize her. Their hands touched, fingers brushing. Their gazes locked over the little girl's head.

"The doggie has to go home, Brenna," Avery said, lifting her while taking a step back. To Judson, she said, "Thanks again for coming out and checking on the faucet."

"No problem. I'll see you soon. Bye, Brenna."

Once he was in his truck and heading back home, Judson wondered how long he'd have to wait until Avery drove to his ranch. He could only hope that would be the next time he saw her, and that no other accident had him returning to her place.

FOUR DAYS AFTER Judson cleared the ice patch from outside her back door, Avery carefully navigated the snow-plowed highway. She sincerely hoped the road leading to Judson's ranch would be the same. Three people had passed her, each giving her a friendly toot of their horn or wave as they went by.

"What do you think, Brenna?" Avery asked, with a quick peek at her daughter secure in her car seat. She was glad Brenna had grown enough that she faced Avery now. "Should I leave the Georgia license plates on the car so people will know I'm not used to driving in the snow?" She smiled at the garbled, toddler answer.

"You're right, of course. No one will take us seriously about staying here if we cling to the past."

Following the GPS directions she turned left then let out a sigh of relief at finding a paved road. Snow was piled a foot high on either side and extended as far as she could see. It was another aspect to Judson's life as a rancher, she supposed, that he not only bred horses, but had to maintain the ranch property.

When the house came into view, she braked to an abrupt stop. Her eyes went wide. It wasn't the size of the house that surprised her—she'd been in other homes larger and more lavish.

But this home was different. This one was welcoming.

For someone who earned their living by creating graphics

to entice and inspire interest, she knew the value of presentation. Staring at Judson's house, she was overwhelmed with a sense of warmth and homecoming. Because of the memories she had of times spent with her uncle, she was very attached to her cabin, and felt it was more than adequate for the life she planned to make for herself and her daughter. If she stayed in Burton Springs. But Judson's house all but grabbed her by the throat, as if it were a living, breathing thing that could provide peace of mind, invite happiness, promise security.

Offer love.

"Your mama's spent too many late hours writing copy," Avery said to Brenna after she'd taken her out of the car seat.

The walls were rough-hewn logs, the metal roof was green and a wide porch wrapped around both sides of the house. She somehow knew it would extend along the back, as well. At one end, a stone chimney reached up to the sky. Snow covered the ground but she could picture gardens overflowing with a rainbow of marigolds, zinnias, Shasta daisies, lavender, and black-eyed Susans.

She wondered why a single man wanted so much space.

Holding onto a squirming Brenna, Avery walked along the cleared pathway. Skirting the corner of the house, she saw she'd been right and wrong. The deck did span along the back of the house—but it stretched to an enclosed sunroom with wide windows that overlooked the pasture and barn area. There was an upstairs balcony off what she assumed to be the master bedroom. She saw several machines, tractors and the snow plow that had cleared the road leading to his ranch. There were two large barns, with a corral next to one. That's where she spotted Judson.

He stood in the center of the ring, his face shadowed by the brim of his hat. Although the air was cold, he wore only a plaid flannel shirt covered by a leather vest with his jeans and boots.

"Shh," she said to Brenna when she squealed at spotting Judson.

He used one hand to hold a rope connected to the horse, and a long, thin stick in his other hand. She watched as he urged the horse forward with a tug on the rope, then stopped the movement before repeating the process. If, or when, the horse didn't move forward as expected, he tapped the tip of the stick on the horse's belly as incentive. He was so patient, going over the same routine time after time, alternating direction but not speed. She couldn't hear the words of command he spoke but she heard the gentle, yet strong tone of his voice. She grimaced in sympathy once when the horse stepped on his foot and she heard his muffled oath. Still, he didn't use the stick for anything more than an occasional gentle prod and his voice continued that firm yet coaxing tone.

When he stopped in the middle of the ring and stroked a hand over the horse, she approached.

"Hi. Hi, 'Udson," Brenna called out.

Avery kept a firm grip on her squirming daughter, preventing her from getting down. "No, Brenna. Stay here."

"Horsie."

"This is Gracie." Judson stroked the horse while he looked at them. "She's not following orders too well from her owner, so I'm working with her. I'm not sure how she'd react to the little one."

Avery took a reflexive step backward. "Brenna," she said in her calmest voice. She took Brenna's hand in hers, rubbing her thumb over the palm. "You have to be quiet or you'll scare the horse."

"Horsie."

"Yes, I know."

"Doggie?"

"Ginger's in the house," Judson said, continuing to stroke the horse. "It's cold out here. Why don't you go on in. I'll be right there. Stay back," he said suddenly, sharply enough that Avery took a reflexive step back.

That was when she noticed the man who'd come around the corner of the barn. He wore jeans, and a flannel shirt, covered by an open denim coat, and boots. His hair was the same dark, rich color and fullness as Judson's. A lit cigarette hung from the corner of his mouth.

"Hi," Brenna called out, waving a hand at the older man.

For some reason, her previously shy daughter had become very friendly since moving to Montana. With his lips curving slightly, the man who was so obviously Judson's father lifted a fingertip to the brim of his hat, but remained silent.

"I told you my father's a heavy smoker," Judson said as his father took the cigarette out of his mouth, crushing it on a raised boot heel before putting the butt in his back pocket. "It's best if he keeps his distance from Brenna. She shouldn't be breathing in second-hand smoke."

"Judson, we're outside."

She nearly took another step back when he whipped his gaze around to her. Gone was the easygoing, flirtatious man who'd charmed both her and her daughter. Here was a man intent and focused on believing he was right.

"It doesn't matter. Go on inside, Avery. You're shivering."

She was, but not because of the cold. At least not the cold weather. It was the coldness in his voice when he spoke of his father—the man who stood by and accepted the words his son threw out. Avery might not have had the closest relationship with her parents but she'd never spoken about them with the level of cold dismissal she'd heard in Judson's tone. Then she recalled how he'd asked the doctor to come out and check on him. Could it be that he used anger to hide his fear of losing his father?

How many times during the long years of nursing her father had she wavered between being grateful for time with him and resenting the effort spent on a man who so rarely found anything right in what she did for him.

"Maybe it's better if we come back another time."

"No, ma'am," said Judson's father. "I'll get out of the way." With a glance toward his son, he turned on his heel and disappeared behind the barn.

"Bye-bye," Brenna said, waving again.

"I'd really like you to stay," Judson said. "Just give me a few minutes to get Gracie back in her stall. There's milk and . . ." For the first time, he smiled. "C-o-o-k-i-e-s," he spelled. "In the pantry. There's a door on the left side of the deck. It leads right into the mudroom. Make yourself at home."

"Make yourself at home," Avery repeated to Brenna as she stopped by her SUV to retrieve the bag holding toys and other assorted items Brenna might need. "How am I supposed to do that in a stranger's house?" Using her hip to shut the door, she grinned when Brenna answered, "Doggie."

"Okay, we'll go see the doggie. I admit, I'm curious about the inside of the house."

When she stepped into the mudroom, she knew she wasn't going to be disappointed. While the room was larger than hers, he also had a bench with baskets underneath and hooks above, for boots, coats, and hats. Avery stripped Brenna out of her coat, then removed hers, grabbing Brenna's hand before she could run off.

"Stay with me, sweetheart."

"Doggie."

From the doorway, she could see through the dining room and into the kitchen. Ginger rose from her bed, her tail wagging as she watched them. Brenna tugged and Avery let go, watching with a slight pinch in her chest as her daughter ran over to give the dog a hug. Trusting in a way she didn't think she ever had with anyone before, pet or human, Avery glanced away from the dog and Brenna and took in the house.

The dining room they'd passed through had been spacious with a simple table and six chairs. French doors divided the dining room from the kitchen, which was bright and open, with the expected stainless appliances and a mile of countertops. Angled in the far corner was a banquette table with benches cushioned in a nubby fabric the same deep blue as she had used in her kitchen.

She spun around, like a kid caught with her hand in the cookie jar, when she heard the mudroom door slam shut. Sudden nerves had her moving toward Brenna, who Avery now noticed, was playing in the dog's water dish.

"Brenna, no, that's for the dog."

"Bath?"

"No." Avery choked on a laugh. Grabbing a paper towel

from the roll on the counter, she sat on the floor next to a very patient Ginger and lifted Brenna onto her lap. "The water is for the doggie," she explained, drying off her hand. "Not for little girls."

When she felt his presence—there was quite simply no other way to describe it—she looked up to find Judson staring at them. The stark hunger she saw in his gaze had nothing to do with food. She couldn't even say it involved desire, or at least not entirely. It was like the entire package. A deep need to come home and find someone waiting for him, someone to share the day's events with. Someone to share duties and laughter along with the worry and the doubts of parenting.

Everything she'd always longed for and done without her entire life.

"Did you fall?"

"No." She swallowed to try and ease the dryness in her throat. "Uhm, Brenna was playing in Ginger's water bowl. I was just wiping up the spill." She glanced down at the hardwood floor. "I don't think there's any damage."

"A little water's not going to hurt the floor," he said.

"Speaking of water." Avery kept her head ducked as she ran the towel over the floor. "Daniel Gaines called me. Said he'd heard I'd had some trouble with a faucet."

"He didn't hear it from me."

"I didn't think so. He offered to come over and make sure everything around the house was fine so that I didn't have any other trouble. He was perfectly nice. Until I told him you'd helped me with the ice the leaking faucet had created."

Judson sat beside her and, as was already becoming her habit, Brenna immediately climbed onto his lap. "How did he react to that?"

She looked up at him. "Pretty much the same way you did when you heard he'd come by to plow my road. He cautioned me about you, implying you were interested in buying my land."

"I am."

"I know that. But there was something about the way he

talked about you that just made me mad. At least you've been honest about it."

"I'm getting fitted for my halo tomorrow."

Avery laughed. "You're not that good."

"Wanna bet? What I've done has shot me to the top of Santa's *nice* list. Come see."

Holding Brenna, he stood and offered Avery a hand. Hers felt small in his, protected by the strength of his fingers closing around hers, supporting as he easily helped her to her feet and led them into the main room.

"Oh, Judson," she said as he walked toward a wicker basket overflowing with toys.

"I ordered some things for the Christmas toy drive and I decided to get a few extras for whenever you came to visit."

He set Brenna down and she immediately pulled everything out of the basket. A plastic car with shapes carved into the sides for blocks to fit through, and stuffed animals, including a dog that looked like a young Ginger, was followed by a picnic basket with plastic food and a pink tea party set.

"Don't worry," Judson said, walking over to the black leather recliner that matched the two sofas on the other side of the room and pulling out a bag from behind them. "I didn't forget about you."

"What?"

"Don't get too excited. For all you know, it's a bag of coal."

She accepted the gift bag he offered. "Feels heavy enough." She dug through the tissue paper and drew out a rectangular box. "Something's not going to jump out at me, is it?"

"Nope. I promise."

Opening the box, she pulled out a Santa figurine dressed in jeans, boots, hat and holding a rope.

"When I saw it, I knew I had to get it for your first Montana Christmas," he said, his smile as bright and eager as a young boy's on Christmas morning.

"Thank you," she whispered. Then, to her disbelief, she rose on her toes and kissed his cheek.

In that moment, the air stilled, her heart calmed, their

surroundings faded. It had been so long since she'd touched a man, even in so innocent a manner. He didn't reach for her, didn't shift his face for a deeper kiss. So why did it feel as if the moment had shifted from friendly to . . .more?

She mentally shook her head. That wasn't possible. She was simply overreacting to a thoughtful gesture after so much time on her own.

"Well," she said, carefully returning the Santa into the box. "With you already started on your shopping, I'm surprised you don't have your tree up."

"I don't decorate for Christmas."

"What?"

She glanced around the spacious room, taking in the wood wainscotting, the large fireplace with a raised hearth. And there, between the two windows overlooking his land, was the perfect spot for a brightly lit Christmas tree. It was something she still needed to pick up for herself. One of the ways she intended to make her life different here in Montana was by giving Brenna an old-fashioned Christmas. There would be no designer inspired and decorated tree ever again in her home.

"Why not?" she asked, sending Brenna a quick glance before turning back to Judson.

"Why would I? It's just me living here."

"You buy toys for the toy drive, and gifts for someone you hardly know, you offer horse drawn carriage rides during the Christmas season . . . And yet you don't decorate this beautiful house. Judson, I have to say that's a crime."

"What would you do?" he asked, extending a hand to encompass the room.

"I'd start with a big tree between these two windows." She walked over, her back to the wall, her arms spread wide to indicate how large a tree the room could support. "If you've never decorated, then I guess you don't have a stash of ornaments stored in the attic?" He shook his head. "I'm picking up some when they catch my attention."

"You mean like you did in Audra's studio?"

"Yes, I want the ornaments I choose to have meaning. They

will always be a reminder of my Christmas here."

"You make it sound like you only plan on being here for one Christmas."

"I honestly don't know. And I'm not going to think about it until after the first of the year. But I promise that whatever I decide, you'll be the first I tell." She frowned when he said nothing. "You don't think that's fair?"

"It's more than fair. What isn't fair is that you're making it hard for me to know what I want that decision to be."

"I'm not sure I understand."

He stepped closer. "I want your land, but I'm not sure that I like knowing I'll only get it if you leave. I like you, Avery. More than I have liked any woman in some time."

She was speechless. She'd felt, of course, that tug of attraction. She just hadn't expected him to be so upfront about the issue. "I'm not sure what to say."

His lips curved slightly. "Well, as you're fond of saying, let's enjoy Christmas first. Now, how would you decorate this mythical tree of mine?"

"Uhm, you could go with classic white and silver balls in various sizes as fill-in while you collect ornaments that have meaning for you." She walked over to the fireplace, ran a hand over the live edge wood of the mantel. "Garland draped on the mantel. And stockings of course."

"Of course."

"I'd toss colorful lap blankets over the backs of the sofas. Red and white candles throughout the house, even though I'd have to wait a year or so before I could trust Brenna around them."

"Sold. When will you come by and put it all together?"

She laughed. "First you offer me a job designing your website and a logo, and now you want to hire me as your Christmas decorator?"

"I like your ideas."

So did she. Too much.

"I'm sure if you put your mind to it, you can handle it yourself."

"I could." He walked to her. "But I'd rather have you here, doing it with me." While she stared at him, he drew her into his arms and began swaying. "We could have Christmas music playing, a fire in the fireplace, chilled wine with cheese and crackers while we decorate the tree. After, Brenna will be asleep upstairs, dreaming of all the toys Santa will bring her." He brought her closer as his voice lowered to a whisper. "And with just the tree lights on, we can dance like we are now."

Her heart pounded, her throat grew dry and she ached in a way she hadn't in months, in years. The picture he painted was so much more vivid and enticing than the one she'd described. It offered more than Christmas. It was, as she'd thought when he entered the kitchen a short time earlier, the entire package—a family holiday.

The bond of doing something together, the making of memories, the romanticism of the images he described, made her heart yearn for what she'd never had. And it made her consider taking a chance on what the future might hold. Even if only short-term.

"Get the tree," she said. "Then we'll dance."

Chapter Five

"WERE YOU SERIOUS about the website and logo?" Avery asked, smiling as Brenna offered tea to the dog. "Or was that a ploy to get me over here to decorate your house for Christmas?"

From where they sat on the floor, Judson accepted, and drank from his cup while Brenna watched. "Thank you, that was delicious," he said and returned the tiny cup. "I'd like a website that's more than the cut and dry stuff I've got on there now."

"It is pretty basic."

"Checked it out, did you?"

"Of course." From the bag she'd brought along, she pulled out a notepad and pencil. "Why do you concentrate on breeding quarter horses?"

"It's the most versatile horse breed. It can be used for ranch work, rodeos use them for barrel racing, calf roping and as a cutting horse. Some quarter horses have even been trained in dressage and show jumping."

"I had no idea."

He grinned. "How many horses were you around in Georgia?"

"You've got me there." Ginger nosed Brenna away from climbing the stairs.

"Have you ever ridden?"

"Uncle Alex took me on my first ride the summer after I turned nine. I was nervous, but I was determined not to fall."

"Stubborn."

"That too. Mostly, I wanted him to be proud of me."

Judson took her hand. "He must have been proud or he wouldn't have left you his land."

"It's the reason I moved here." She smiled ruefully. "Well, that and because my ex-husband tried to screw me out of keeping the property."

"Stubborn," Judson repeated, this time making it sound like a compliment. "And cautious."

"I like the sound of cautious better. I don't know if Montana is the place for me and Brenna long-term. My business means I can work pretty much anywhere and selling the land would give me financial security."

"But?"

"Everyone's made me feel so welcome. Maybe I'm more tender after the divorce than I thought, but it's nice to have genuine friends rather than acquaintances looking to make the right connections."

"So, you don't miss Georgia?"

"No. My college roommate tried to talk me into moving to New York, but I'm not sure that's where I want to raise Brenna." She smiled, remembering her last conversation with Londyn. "Besides, the snow is prettier here than in New York."

"Your Christmas streak is showing again."

"Please. What you've heard me talk about is the tip of the iceberg. Or the Christmas tree, in this case."

"Why is it so important to you?"

She glanced across the room, smiled at discovering Brenna and Ginger asleep next to each other. "It's the classic case of wanting to give my daughter everything I never had." She looked back at him. "My parents were older, well-educated. They didn't believe in telling me what they called lies about the holiday season. I want to see the glow in Brenna's eyes when she wakes up to all the lights and decorations, hear the innocent joy in her voice as she talks about Santa, and make memories while singing Christmas carols or making cookies."

He leaned forward, and she caught the glimmer of humor in his eyes. "What kind of Christmas cookies?"

"Ah, now I understand where this conversation is leading."

"My mom used to make these red and white cookies in the shape of a candy cane. Do you know how to make them?"

She looked at him, secretly enjoying this side of him. "If I promise to find the recipe, will you help me make them?"

"Your house or mine?" he asked.

"Are you kidding?" She waved her free hand over her shoulder. "With the kind of kitchen you have? It's a no-brainer."

"So, you're using me for my kitchen space."

"You're one to talk. You're using me for cookies."

"Only until I've tasted your cookies."

"I'll have you know I kill at baking cookies."

"I'll be the judge of that."

"Which means you plan to eat them as soon as they come out of the oven."

"It's the best way to eat cookies."

"Cookies."

They both turned to discover Brenna awake and walking toward them. "Hey, sweetie," Avery crooned, holding out her arms. "Did you have a good nap?"

"Cookies."

"I've always admired a female who knows what she wants and isn't afraid to ask for it," Judson said, rising and offering Avery his hand to give her a lift.

"I just bet you do."

"I'm talking about cookies." He started for the kitchen. "Okay, Brenna. Let's see what I have to get us by until your mom shows off her baking skills."

"But she hasn't had lunch."

"Consider it one of your new traditions that there are no food rules during the Christmas season."

"My traditions? Or one that happens to fit your needs at the moment?"

He stopped and looked down at her in that way he had that set her heart racing. "I have many needs," he whispered. Just when she thought he might kiss her, he walked over to a barn-type of sliding door and opened it, revealing a pantry half the size of her current kitchen. Not only were there food staples stored inside but there were also a multitude of small appliances and serving dishes.

"If I screw up the cookie recipe, I'll only have myself to blame."

"Cookie, Mama."

Faced with two pleading faces, she gave up and reached for a familiar package. "All right. Let's have cookies."

Avery limited Brenna to three cookies, while Judson, between answering and sending texts on his phone, ate seven. Making herself at home, she searched through his refrigerator and found cheese that she sliced into thin strips.

"See? Those cookies didn't spoil her appetite at all," Judson said, looking at his phone when it buzzed with a text.

"I'm sorry if we're keeping you from something. Brenna, no, don't give the dog any cheese." Avery stood and went to the sink to wet a paper towel. "As soon as I clean everything up, we'll leave."

His big hand covered hers. "You're not keeping me from anything." He held up his phone. "It's just my father," he explained. "This is how we communicate. He has the, uh, animal that you came out here to see, ready."

"Ready for what?"

"Her first ride."

Avery felt a knee-jerk impulse to refuse, to claim Brenna was too small and young. Then, she recalled the thrill of her first ride. She studied Judson, the patience in his gaze as he waited for her reply, the strength of the arms that would hold her daughter. How was it that she trusted this man she'd only known a handful of days with the most precious thing in her life?

With a nod, they went to the mudroom for coats, hats, and shoes. "Remember," she told Brenna as they walked outside. "You have to be careful and go slow."

She looked up and locked gazes with Judson, who stood by a horse with black and white coloring. He looked so calm and confident. Inspired, she dug in her pocket for her phone and took a couple of quick photos.

"For the website," she explained as he walked to her, one gloved hand holding the reins of the horse. Somehow, before she could guess his intention—or thwart it—he eased Brenna away from her.

Judson grinned. "Take your picture, Mama," he said in a

soothing tone as he took Brenna's hand and showed her how to stroke the horse.

Avery recognized this moment was priceless, as far as PR was concerned, so she took several shots. Getting into the spirit of the moment, she moved on to take photos of the grounds, the barn, the other horses. When she spotted Judson's father with one foot braced against the side of the corral, cigarette smoke curling up and around the brim of his hat, she took a couple of him.

When he stiffened, tossing the cigarette to the ground, and grinding it with the heel of his boot, she lowered the phone. "I'm sorry. I got caught up." She took a few steps closer. "I'm Avery, Avery McClain. Judson asked me to help him set up a website for the ranch."

"He's going to want you to keep your distance."

"I'm self-employed, Mr. Ford. That means I decide what I do or don't do."

His quick laugh ended with a cough. "It's Hodge, ma'am. That's a right pretty girl you've got there. My Roberta . . .." He stared off into the distance. "She hoped to have a baby girl." He looked back. "It wasn't anything against Judson."

"I'd like to have another baby someday," she said, surprising herself by voicing the admission to a stranger. "Judson was worried about you. The other day, when he sent the doctor out to check on you."

"Worrying doesn't change a thing."

"Maybe not. Are you going to tell me you never worried about Judson?" She smiled a little when he looked at her.

"The boy had the usual scrapes and cuts you get on a ranch."

"You must be proud of what he's built here."

"He does the work." He reached in his coat pocket, as if for another cigarette. Only he dropped his hand without one. "It's a good place." He nodded in the direction of the corral. "Your little girl's taken with it."

Avery glanced over her shoulder. Brenna sat on Judson's lap as they rode the horse in a slow circle around the perimeter of the fenced area. Pride filled her at the way her daughter sat so still, even as she laughed with delight.

Avery lifted her cellphone, taking photos of Brenna before shifting to Judson.

His lips were curved as they moved while he obviously spoke. His eyes constantly scanned the surroundings for any obstacles. His body was relaxed and yet she had no doubt he was prepared to move if necessary.

He looked so sure, not cocky but confident of his skill and ability. She'd observed it so often in him. Whether he soothed her sleepy daughter, shoveled snow, or held her hand while they talked, he moved with purpose. Is that why she found him so compelling? Because she was at a transitional time of her life and he seemed so steady?

Avery lifted a hand to rub at her temples.

"He'll be careful with her," Hodge said.

"I know," she said. The problem was, it wasn't her daughter in danger of being hurt.

THE TOWN LOOKED like a Christmas card.

Wreaths with bright red or silver bows hung from every streetlight. Storefront windows were decorated to within an inch of their display space. Vendors lined the cordoned-off street, filling the area with the scent of warmed chestnuts and popcorn to go along with the smells of hot chocolate and coffee. The high school choir sang carols as they meandered through the crowd. People, dressed in heavy coats against the night cold and light snow, gathered in groups to talk or hurried by on their way to one of the many entertainment booths set up in the main square. A long line of children waited for a chance to sit on Santa's lap.

Avery had yet to head towards where Judson was giving his horse drawn wagon rides.

"Lights, Mama."

"Yes, I see."

"We lights."

"We have lights," Avery agreed with a smile as they continued walking. Since she'd strung multi-colored lights on their

Christmas tree three days earlier, Brenna had become obsessed with them, asking for more throughout the house.

She stopped at one vendor, buying three Christmas-themed hair bows for Brenna. At another booth showcasing personalized Christmas ornaments, she selected a wooden horse. While waiting for the young girl to add Brenna's name, she spotted a pewter cowboy hat. Unable to resist, she bought it for Judson.

"Doing some Christmas shopping?"

From where she'd been selecting two hand-knitted scarves at a booth sponsored by the local women's shelter, Avery looked over at Daniel Gaines. Beside him stood a slim young girl dressed in jeans and a sweater, the ends of her blond hair just showing beneath her cowboy hat.

"Hello, Daniel." From her peripheral vision, she saw Rhonda Johnson, her coat buttoned up to the chin, and wrapped up in one of the scarves on sale, lower her hand to beneath the counter. "Yes, I like to shop local whenever I can."

"Looks like you could use an extra hand," he said as Avery juggled her bags and Brenna, trying to pull her wallet out of her coat pocket. He nodded toward the girl at his side. "This is my daughter, Frances."

"Frankie," she corrected, earning a look from her father. "Uhm, I can hold her."

Even if she'd been inclined, and if Brenna hadn't immediately buried her face into her shoulder, Avery wouldn't have handed her over to the girl who obviously had no interest in small children.

"Thanks, but as you can see, she's shy."

He took a step closer. "Why don't I treat you to some hot chocolate and we can all get to know each other better."

"There you are."

Avery sighed in relief as Audra Montgomery walked up to them.

"We've been looking for you. Can I?" With a mother's ease, Audra scooped Brenna out of Avery's arms. "Oh," she sighed, smiling over her shoulder at her husband, Carter, standing behind her.

"Gaines," he addressed the other man, who nodded. "Didn't expect to run into you tonight."

"Just being neighborly." He smiled at Avery, then glared at his daughter when she mumbled something under her breath. "And I wanted to make sure Avery hasn't had any more trouble at her place."

"None," she answered.

"That's good. Remember you can call me anytime if you need help." He nodded at Carter, then tipped the brim of his hat at Audra. "We'll just be on our way."

"What kind of trouble was he talking about?" Carter asked.

Avery explained about the water faucet. "You be careful," Rhonda said. "He's a sneaky bas . . ." She stopped, looking at the small faces around her. "Well, you just be careful."

"Judson's already warned me about him."

"'Udson," Brenna said, clapping her hands.

"Well, well," Rhonda remarked with a smirk. "Looks like Judson's got an admirer."

"Mostly she likes his dog."

"Doggie," Brenna cried. "An' horsie."

"He's driving the Christmas wagon tonight. You should go for a ride," Rhonda said with a wicked grin that had Avery's cheeks firing.

"We were just going there ourselves," Audra said. "Why don't you join us?"

"I don't want to intrude on your family time."

"I'd feel better if you were with us," Carter said, looking in the direction Gaines and his daughter had gone.

"I'll keep an eye on your bags for you," Rhonda offered.

Audra reached for Brenna's hand. "Want to go for a ride, sweetie?"

Avery walked beside Bradley, the for-now middle Montgomery boy. "Did you see Santa?" she asked.

He gave her the surprisingly short list of what he'd asked Santa for before he tugged on her hand. Bending down, he whispered. "That's not the real Santa. It's Mr. Anderson. But don't worry. He has a real beard so your little girl will probably think it's the real Santa."

"You're right, she won't know the difference. I just want a picture of her sitting on his lap."

A greedy light came into his green eyes. "Can she eat candy canes?"

"It might be best if she doesn't. Know someone I can give hers to?"

She was still smiling as she walked around a corner and spotted Judson standing beside a wagon decorated with a wreath at either end of a leather strap holding silver bells. Battery powered lanterns hung from each side, adding a warm glow to the interior of the back seating area.

Judson wore his usual cowboy hat, but she could still make out the lines of his face under the shadow of the brim. His lips curved into a tempting smile when he saw her. For one long heartbeat, she could almost imagine no one else was around. The pleasure of seeing him unsettled her, even as a warm thrill wound around her center.

"Just in time for the last ride of the night." He held out a gloved hand. "Sit up here."

Avery shifted, realizing that while she'd been staring at Judson like a star-struck teenager, all the seats in the wagon had filled. Brenna sat on the floor of the wagon with the Montgomery boys, playing with their cars and trucks.

"Don't worry," Audra called out from where she snuggled against her husband. "We'll all keep an eye on her."

Judson's strong hand closed around hers as he guided her onto the front bench seat. Once he had a wool blanket spread over them, he flipped a switch and *Dashing Through the Snow* played through hidden speakers.

"It's a new addition. Easier than using my phone." With a flick of the reins, also lined with silver bells, he urged the horses moving in a slow walk.

"Having a good time tonight?" he asked.

"It's wonderful. The town is so pretty. The tree lighting was sweet, especially when the mayor repeated the story of Van proposing to Gabriella on Christmas Eve before insisting they be the ones to flip the switch on the lights. And that tree-topper Van made? Absolutely stunning. There are so many vendors with such interesting things."

He chuckled when she finally quit talking. "I'm surprised you don't have a handful of bags."

"I did. Rhonda offered to keep them for me."

"Find any memorable Christmas ornaments during your shopping?"

She sent him a shy smile. "Maybe if you put up a tree, you'd find out. I happen to know the high school has a good selection. In fact, for a small additional fee, a couple of boys will deliver and set it up in the house for you."

"Will you help me pick one out?"

"Seriously?" she asked just, as if in a movie, *Rocking Around the Christmas Tree* came through the speakers.

"I haven't had much luck getting into the Christmas spirit the last couple of years. Spending time with you and Brenna has made me realize what I've been missing."

"You're thinking about cookies again," she teased.

"I'm thinking about a lot of things."

Even as she passed it off as flirting, a ribbon of anticipation twisted through her.

"Here."

Startled she accepted the reins before she realized what he was doing. "Wait, I've never driven a wagon before."

"It's not so different from guiding a horse." He slid an arm around her waist so he could cover her hands with his. "The horses know where to go." As he nudged her to flick or pull back when needed, she felt herself relax in his embrace. "You're doing fine," he said, his voice low. "Just enjoy the ride."

"Are you sure you trust me?"

"I trust my instincts." He gave her a light hug. "They're working fine right now."

"How often has that line worked for you?"

"That depends." He looked down at her, his face shadowed by the brim of his hat and yet she felt the heat of his gaze. "On whether or not you'll let me kiss you before the night's over."

Avery gratefully relinquished her hold on the reins as they returned to the starting point. Once Judson had the horses stopped, she looked over her shoulder, searching for her daughter. She'd hardly given Brenna a thought.

"We're going to end the night with pie at Tammy's," Audra said, folding the wool blanket she'd used on the ride. "Why don't we take Brenna with us and you keep Judson company as he unloads the wagon. When you're done, come join us."

Since it was more statement than question, Avery remained silent as everyone walked away. "Not very subtle, is she?"

Judson said nothing as he urged the horses forward. His silence continued as they rode past the thinning crowd before turning down a street and stopping behind the feed store. He stopped the wagon, then turned to her.

She saw his intent in his eyes—after all, he'd warned her that he wanted to kiss her. She knew she could break away and avoid the complication, only she didn't want to. Maybe it was the romance of the night, maybe it was simply because it had been so long since she'd felt desirable...she didn't know. But she did know that she wanted to feel his mouth on hers. She wanted, even if only for this one time, to feel a rush of desire, and to know that he felt it as well.

His mouth covered hers, softly but with purpose and, oh yes, the appealing hint of passion. His hands reached for hers and held them. Just held them. He didn't make any move she'd have to counter, so she could relax and indulge in the sensation of heat spreading throughout her body.

Finally, with a long exhale, he drew away.

"This Christmas thing might not be so bad after all."

Laughter rumbled in her throat as she pressed her forehead to his. In the distance, she could hear the murmur of conversation, the Christmas carols being sung by a roving quartet, the cheerful greeting of the man dressed as Santa, inviting children to come and sit on his lap.

"I need to get back to Brenna," Avery murmured.

"Stay with me." She eased away, not sure what he was asking. "Stay with me while I tend to the horses."

She nodded.

Afterward, he held her hand as they walked to the booth where Rhonda and another woman were packing up the unsold items.

"I was wondering if you'd gotten lost." Rhonda looked pointedly at their joined hands. "Guess not."

Rhonda wasn't the only one to notice them holding hands. As they walked to the diner, they got more than a few looks from passersby. Within a few minutes, they arrived. The bell above the open door rang, and the warmth and scents of the room welcomed them. Avery smiled when she spotted Brenna sitting in a booster seat next to Audra, melted ice cream covering her face.

She spent the next hour enjoying the company of people she was coming to think of as friends . . . and the undercurrent of attraction she was feeling for the man who sat beside her. With a mother's timing, Audra stopped her boys before a fight erupted.

"Time to get everyone home," Audra said.

"Pie's on me," Judson said, drawing bills out of his pocket and tossing them on the table while kids complained as they had faces and hands wiped clean.

"Avery, why don't we follow you home?" Carter asked. They all stepped outside just as Daniel Gaines drove by. "I'd feel better knowing you got there safely."

"What happened?" Judson asked.

"Daniel stopped to say hello while I was shopping. His daughter was with him."

"And you didn't tell me?"

"I forgot all about it."

He looked at Carter. "I'll follow her home."

When he had Brenna safely tucked in her car seat, Judson opened her door. "I'll be right behind you."

"Really, Judson, I'm sure everything will be fine." She sighed when he said nothing, but simply looked in the back window at her sleeping daughter. "Okay . . . Fine."

Chapter Six

JUDSON DIDN'T seriously believe Daniel Gaines would do anything to Avery or her house tonight. Not after being seen talking to her in town. Still, he wasn't willing to take the chance.

Even when he parked behind her SUV at her house, and he could tell by her body language that she was angry, he didn't give a flip.

He didn't try to take a sleeping Brenna from her, but instead held out a hand for her keys so he could unlock the door. Once inside, he flicked a glance over at the Christmas tree, and turned the lights on while he searched through the rooms. He shook off any sense of impropriety when he entered Avery's bedroom, although it was impossible not to imagine her snuggled beneath the thick comforter. He turned when he heard her walk into the bedroom.

"I didn't find any sign of anyone being here."

"We saw Daniel leave. There wasn't time for him to do anything."

His chest ached from trying to keep his breathing level. His hands closed into tight fists. "I couldn't just walk away. Not again."

Her gaze narrowed, the anger fading beneath the concern. "Judson? What's this really all about?"

He could have offered any number of excuses. He could have related incidents where Daniel had been suspected of wrongdoing, but it hadn't been proven. He could have taken her in his arms and kissed away the tension between them.

"I haven't told you the whole story about my wife's death."

She stared at him a long moment before she reached for his hand. Linking fingers, she led them past the Christmas tree and into the kitchen. "Sit." He did as she asked, then watched as she filled a kettle and put it on the stovetop. Even in slacks, he admired the long line of her legs when she reached into a cabinet to get the tea and mugs. He relaxed a little, smiling when he saw the inscription on the cups: *I heart Santa.*

When she placed a plate of cookies on the table, he had to dig deep to maintain his composure.

They were the red and white candy cane shaped cookies he'd mentioned. Some of these were redder, or whiter, in color rather than being split evenly. Some were even misshapen.

"I need to work on getting the shape and color distribution right."

"Still, they taste as good as I remember," he said after plopping a whole one in his mouth. He ate three more as she filled the mugs with peppermint tea. While he'd been given milk rather than tea, or the coffee he would prefer if he was being honest, the scenario reminded him of sitting with his mother in the kitchen. So, when Avery set the mug before him, he took a sip, hoping to ease the sudden dryness in his throat.

She didn't rush, didn't ask questions. She ignored the cookies while blowing a cooling breath on her tea. He reached for another cookie, more to keep his hands busy than out of hunger.

"I told you that Melanie was hit by a driver when she was out for a run. What I didn't say was that she'd gone on the run because we'd been fighting." He paused, surprised how much it still hurt. So, he rushed through the words, hoping to lessen the ache. "I'd been telling her I wanted to move back here and start the family we'd always talked about having. That's when she told me no, she wasn't going to let anything get in her way of making the Olympic team. She'd had her tubes tied while I was out of town."

Avery curled her hand on his arm. He shook his head.

"I know there are other ways to have a family, adoption for one. But she knew how badly I wanted kids. And I felt blindsided that she'd gone behind my back. So, I stormed out of the apartment without a word and walked for a while before stopping at a bar. When I got a call from her, I ignored it." He drank some tea. "It rang two other times before I finally answered. It was a nurse calling from her phone to tell me about the accident.

By the time I got to the hospital, she was gone."

"You blame yourself."

"If I'd stayed, she wouldn't have been out on a run."

"Are you sure?"

He blinked. He'd never considered that Melanie would have gone for that run anyway. After all, running was what she'd lived for. What she'd loved more than him or their life together.

"You might be right," he said. "Still, I couldn't just let you come home alone tonight. What if Daniel had been here? Or if he'd had someone waiting here to attack you?"

"For a piece of land?"

"That's part of it. I told you, it's natural for a rancher to always want more land, and yours has the added benefit of a water source. Daniel isn't the kind of man who likes being told no." He reached for her hand. "You need to be careful."

She shivered. "Maybe I should sell and move."

Judson wasn't as ruthless as he'd heard Daniel could be, but in the past, he also hadn't been above using every advantage to reach his goal. Still, he found it hard to encourage Avery to sell her land and move away. Or maybe it was that he didn't like the thought of her leaving. It was something he would have to think about. In the meantime, he'd do what he could to keep her close.

"You can't leave."

"Is that so?"

"Yes. If you do, I'll have no reason to put up a Christmas tree."

"You really are going to do it?"

"If you help." When she smiled, he stood. "Can I take some of these cookies home?"

"Let me put some in a bag for you."

She followed him and leaned on the door as he walked out onto the back porch. "Judson, will you call me when you get home? Concern works both ways," she added when he hesitated.

"I will. Lock up now."

He waited until she did so before he drove away. Arriving home, he held out until he had stripped off his boots, coat and hat and gave Ginger a hello rub before he reached for his phone.

"Made it," he said when she answered his call.

"Good."

He heard the relief in her voice and couldn't recall the last time someone had worried about him. "I didn't keep you up, did I?"

"No. I couldn't settle after you left so I decided to work on the design I was invited to submit for a national marketing campaign. I have to complete it before the end of the year."

"Another deadline."

"Yes," she said after a brief pause.

"Does that mean you won't have time to help me look for a Christmas tree tomorrow?"

"Are you kidding? And give you time to change your mind?"

"What time should I pick you up?"

"It's better if I drive to your ranch. I have the car seat Brenna needs."

"Come whenever you want."

"Judson? I enjoyed the wagon ride tonight."

"So did I. Don't work too late, Avery."

"I won't."

After he hung up, he went outside while Ginger made her last round of the night. He watched her sniff, even tossed a ball a few times for her. Turning, he stared at his house.

A single light glowed in the kitchen while the rest of the house waited in darkness. He thought of Avery's house, of sitting in her small kitchen lit only by the lights on her Christmas tree, enveloped by the scent of peppermint from the tea she'd brewed and the cookies she'd made.

His mind repeated her belief that he should let go of the guilt for not preventing Melanie from going on that final run. Funny how one person could say something others had, but for some reason, it rooted stronger. And because it had, he was more determined than ever to keep Avery and Brenna safe.

AVERY HAD NO problem finding excuses for delaying her arrival at Judson's ranch the next day. While she could tell herself that helping him pick a Christmas tree was just a neighborly gesture, she couldn't forget their kiss.

Plus, she'd made the mistake of telling Brenna where they were going.

"Doggie. Horsie."

"Brenna." Avery lifted fingertips to rub at her temple. "Don't kick the back of Mama's seat."

When the house and barns came into view, Brenna's squeals of delight added pressure to Avery's muddled thoughts. While she needed to keep reminding herself that he wanted her land, she couldn't deny she enjoyed his company. She'd learned she couldn't dictate the future. So, she would appreciate the present, and the joy of the Christmas season, as much as possible.

Her heart kicked a little when Judson came around the side of the barn, headed their way, Ginger at his side.

"Just in time," he said as Avery stepped out of the SUV. He opened the rear door and lifted Brenna from her car seat, smothering her face with kisses and eliciting giggles before setting her down so she could hug Ginger.

They let Brenna run off some energy, then secured her in the car seat again and drove to the high school tree lot.

Once there, Judson opened the back door of the SUV and unfastened her. "Don't worry. I've got her," Judson said, settling Brenna on his shoulders, with one broad hand spread across her back, and the other clasping her legs on his chest to hold her steady. "It'll be easier than pushing the stroller around the trees."

"Lights," Brenna said, clapping her hands.

For more than half an hour, they walked up and down the rows. It amused Avery that, for someone who claimed he hadn't wanted a tree, Judson proved to be very particular about which one he chose. Finally, he settled on a gorgeous ten-foot-tall Frasier fir.

"How are we going to get this in your house?" she asked as she watched four high school boys load and secure it on top of her SUV.

Just then, Daniel and his daughter approached. "Need a hand?" It unnerved Avery when she realized this was the second time Daniel had seen her and Judson together. It was almost as if he'd been watching them.

"I've got it. Thanks," Judson said.

"Are you picking out your Christmas tree?" Avery asked the girl.

"Why else would we be here?" she answered, then she walked away.

Avery caught the anger in his gaze before Daniel shifted to smile at her. "Perhaps you could join me for dinner and give me some advice on how to deal with a teenage girl." He leaned forward a little and Avery had to lock her knees to stop herself from stepping back. "Of course, I'm just using that as an excuse to ask you to have dinner with me at my ranch. I'd really like to spend some time with you, Avery."

"Tree's secure," Judson said, coming around the back of the SUV. Immediately, Brenna held out her arms for him to take her, inciting another glint of anger in Daniel's gaze.

"Sorry to rush off, Daniel, but Gabriella and Van are meeting us at the house to help unload the tree. They're staying for dinner so we need to stop by The Market before heading home."

"Daniel," Avery said, not wanting to give the man any reason to be angry with her. "Patience is going to be your best approach with your daughter."

"Then we're all in for some rough times."

As she drove away from the tree lot, she checked her rearview mirror and saw Daniel watching them. She looked at Judson. "When did you talk to Gabriella and Van about coming over?"

He held up his cell phone. "Van," he said when the blacksmith answered. "I have a favor to ask."

An hour later, Avery was in Judson's kitchen, stirring the pot of pasta sauce she had simmering on the stove.

"I offered to cook," Gabriella said from where she sat fingering the thin copper bracelet on her wrist. Outside Van and Judson, along with Hodge, were unstrapping the tree.

"I realize this is store-bought sauce but I could hardly expect you to cook. It's enough that you and Van came over to help Judson with the tree."

"Of course, we came. Neighbors help." Avery turned away from the stove and caught Gabriella's dreamy expression. "The first time I cooked for Van, I used store-bought sauce." She smiled. "Just don't ever tell my Pappa."

"Your secret's safe with me. Wine?" she asked, lifting a bottle of Merlot.

"I'd better not." She looked away. "I'm on call."

Avery frowned. Hadn't Gabriella said something earlier about having a day at home? Then again, the lone doctor in a small town probably had to always be prepared to handle emergencies.

"Need a little help," Judson yelled from the French doors in the great room.

"'Udson," Brenna called out, running towards him.

"I've got it. And her," Gabriella said, scooping Brenna up and carrying her.

Lowering the heat under the pot of pasta sauce, Avery arrived in the great room just as the men pushed the tree through the open doors. Cold air and the scent of pine flooded the room. That was when she realized that while Judson and Van struggled to put the tree in place, Hodge stood outside on the deck.

"Hodge," she said, waving at him. "Come in and close those doors behind you before we all freeze to death."

He didn't say a word. No one spoke. He didn't look at Judson, but he did glance at Brenna. Then he closed the doors, turned, and walked away.

Avery stood there, not sure which man was more stubborn—Judson or his father.

"Oh, Judson," Gabriella said into the silence. "The tree fits perfect there."

"It was Avery's idea." He sent her a teasing smile, but Avery could see it strained the corners of his mouth. "The lights alone are going to cost me a fortune."

"I have a start for you," Avery said. Judson opened the small bag she offered and pulled out the pewter cowboy hat ornament bearing the inscription *Home Is Where You Hang Your Hat*.

"I was hoping you'd change your mind about the tree," she said.

"Thank you." He hung it front and center of the tree, then leaned forward to kiss her.

"Well." Avery swiped hands down her jeans, avoided looking in Van and Gabriella's direction. "Time to eat."

JUDSON LIKED VAN and had a soft spot for Gabriella. But right now, he wished like hell they would leave.

All during the meal, conversation had been easy with lighthearted teasing and shared stories. He appreciated the help Van had given him with the tree. Along with his father, Judson admitted. Now that he thought about it, he'd caught little of the bitter nicotine odor on Hodge's clothes.

Avery and Gabriella got along as if they were old friends. Brenna had thrown only a couple of handfuls of pasta down to Ginger.

"I'm sorry I didn't have time to make any dessert," Avery said, standing to clear the table. "Would you like some coffee at least?"

"Not for me," Gabriella said, smiling at her husband as she rose. "Let me help you."

"No, I've got it. I'm going take some of these leftovers out to Hodge."

"What?"

"For your father." She found a plastic container in the cabinet. "Since he didn't stay to eat with us, I thought I'd take some pasta out to him."

"He's probably already eaten."

"Then he'll have it for tomorrow."

"Avery, you know what I told you about being around him."

"And I'll tell you what I told him." She faced Judson. "I'm self-employed. That means *I* decide what I do or don't do."

"I'll take it to him."

"Now?"

He blew out a breath. "Fine."

"We'll walk out with you," Gabriella said, wrapping Avery in a hug. "Thank you for a lovely dinner."

Avery filled the container as they put on their coats. "I won't be long," Judson said as he held the door open for Van and Gabriella.

"Take your time."

"I love you, Judson," Gabriella said once they'd stepped outside.

"Yeah?" He wiggled his brows at Van, who was winging a tennis ball for Ginger to chase. "Does that mean you're leaving this brute and moving in with me?"

"It's not me you want moving in."

"Setting up a Christmas tree is a far cry from moving in together." He scrubbed the back of his neck. "We've only known each other a week or so."

Gabriella smiled at Van, who stepped over and wrapped an arm around her. "Sometimes that's all it takes." She looked back at Judson. "Does she know you want to buy her land?"

"I told her."

"Good." She leaned forward to kiss his cheek. "Now, go talk to your father."

He scowled. "I'm just taking him the meal."

"Talk to him."

Judson stood still, watching Van open the door for Gabriella, returning their waves as they drove away.

"Let's get this over with," he said to the dog.

Hodge opened the door at Judson's first knock. The two men stood on either side of the doorway, staring at one another. Inside, Judson could make out a recliner with a side table holding a single lamp and, surprisingly, an empty ashtray. The television burst with color from a sci-fi show.

"Avery sent this for you. It's some pasta that she made tonight."

"I already ate supper," Hodge said.

"I told her you probably had. She thought maybe you'd want it tomorrow." Judson frowned at the slight shake to his father's hand as he accepted the container. "You feeling okay?"

His stomach tightened at the hesitation.

"I'm trying."

It took Judson a full two minutes before he made sense of the admission. After more than fifty years of a two-pack a day habit, Hodge Ford was finally trying to stop smoking.

"Why now?"

Hodge turned away, leaving the door open. "No point in heating the outside." Judson closed the door behind him. Hodge put the container in the small refrigerator, then just stood there with his back to Judson.

"I know you blame me. Hell, I am to blame." He cleared his throat. "If I could go back, I'd be the one you lost in that fire."

Judson didn't try to smooth over the remark. How could he, when his father was right? He had carried a chip on his shoulder, and a sting in his heart, since they'd lost his mother.

"She never asked me to quit." Suddenly Hodge turned and faced his son. "I swear if she had, I would have done it."

"So why now?"

"I think seeing that little girl with her mama brought it all back."

Judson thought back to his conversation with Avery just last night. Maybe he couldn't offer his father the level of compassion that she had given him, but he didn't have to add to the weight of pain and guilt on his father's face.

"I won't go near her until I've kicked this."

"Do you need anything?"

"You might want to keep your distance." The ghost of a smile lifted his mouth at one corner. "I'm likely to be hard to be around for a bit."

"What else is new?"

"I know I've disappointed you a lot over the years. I'm sorry." Hodge blew out a long breath and looked away. "I still miss her every damn day." He cleared his throat. "You'd best get back to your place." He smiled a little and bent over to rub Ginger. "Otherwise, that little one's going to be screaming for this one."

"I think they've got a mutual admiration going on."

"It's good for both of them."

Judson walked back into his house to a clean kitchen and the sound of Christmas music. He stepped into the great room to find Avery and Brenna sitting on the floor in front of the bare tree, playing with the blocks he'd bought. Ginger went over and captured Brenna's attention. Avery looked up at him.

"I told you he'd eaten already," he said, sitting cross-legged in front of her. "But he did put it in the refrigerator for tomorrow."

"Everything else okay?"

"He's in a foul mood." He shrugged, deciding not to mention his father's promise to quit smoking. Better to wait a few days and see if he relapsed. "Nothing new there."

"It was nice of him to help you and Van with the tree." She smiled. "I still can't believe you went from not wanting one to picking out the biggest one they had."

"Your Christmas spirit rubbed off on me."

"Glad I could help." She cocked her head. "You know, you could start another Christmas tradition by hosting a party."

"Let's not go overboard."

Brenna ran over, pointed at the tree. "No lights."

"Soon," he answered.

"'Kay."

As she snuggled onto his lap, the weight of her trust took his breath away. Judson looked up to find Avery watching them. There were tears in her eyes but a soft smile curved her lips.

"Christmas is a time to have faith."

SNUGGLING DEEP beneath the covers, Avery woke the next morning in the way she'd fallen asleep—warmed by the memory of Judson's reaction to Brenna's trust.

No doubt about it, her little girl had her first crush. And Avery could hardly blame her.

It wasn't the toys he'd stored at his house for her. It was the time he spent with her, the way he took time to hold her, the way he could make her laugh, and how he made sure she was safe. All things a father should do.

No wonder he'd been hurt and angry when he'd learned about his wife's actions.

He claimed to not particularly care for Christmas, yet he drove a horse-drawn wagon—complete with Christmas carols—every weekend for the town's Christmas festivities. He had given in to her suggestion that he have a Christmas tree—the first one in his house. And he'd asked her to help him decorate. She had to admit, she was looking forward to hanging ornaments and stringing lights, as well as placing greenery throughout the room.

"Mama."

Avery shot up in bed. Brenna's voice hadn't come through the monitor but had echoed down the hallway. She blinked and looked around the room. Where was the faint glow of the night light she kept in the bathroom? Shivering, she threw back the comforter, her breath puffing out as she ran to the bedroom. A slap at the wall switch produced no overhead light. Thankfully there was enough sunlight coming through the window that she could see as she crossed the room.

"Oh, baby," Avery crooned as she snuggled Brenna against her.

"Cold, Mama."

"I know." She snatched up another blanket as she walked into the kitchen where the thermostat didn't respond to her raising the temperature. Opening a cabinet, she drew out a bag of cheese crackers, hoping to distract Brenna. Back in her bedroom, she nestled Brenna in the blanket and comforter.

"We're having a breakfast picnic," she said, trying to keep her voice level as she reached for her cell phone. "Judson," she said when he answered. She smiled when Brenna repeated his name in her unique way. "Do you have power?"

"Sure. Why?" His voice changed with the question. She could hear suspicion, could sense his tension.

"Ours is out. The house is freezing."

"Where are you?"

"In my bed, under the covers."

"Did you look around to see if you saw anything strange?"

"No, I didn't think—"

"Good. Stay where you are. I'm on my way."

Avery entertained Brenna as best she could. The little girl wanted to get out of bed to play with her toys, and turn on the Christmas tree lights. Avery understood. She wanted to have every light in the house blazing too, to have a cup of hot coffee followed by a hotter shower. She wasn't sure who was more relieved when they heard Judson's truck.

"'Udson," Brenna called out when Avery opened the back door.

"Go back inside," Judson said.

"It's just as cold in there as it is out here." She walked around the corner of the house just as he flipped a switch. Instantly she heard the furnace kick to life.

"Breaker was shut off," he explained, closing the cover on the switch.

"I didn't do that."

"Didn't think you did."

"You think Daniel Gaines did this."

"He wasn't happy to see us together at the tree lot."

"So what? Every time I go somewhere or I'm with someone, I have to worry about him sabotaging my house?" she spat out, trembling, no longer from the cold. "He thinks he can scare me off and I'll sell my land to him? I'm sorry, baby," she said when Brenna whimpered, obviously upset by her mother's tone of voice.

"Let's go inside now," Judson said, taking her arm and guiding them back to the house. Inside, he kicked off his boots, but left on his coat. He blew hot breath on his hands and rubbed them together while he walked to her living room. One lamp glowed softly. Kneeling before the fireplace, he checked the flue and turned on the gas, then lit one of the long matches she had in a jar on the hearth. Fire whooshed into the room, bringing the first licks of warmth to help along the furnace.

Avery set Brenna on the floor and turned on the Christmas tree lights.

"I'll talk with Sheriff Owens," Judson said.

"What's the point? All we have are suspicions and no proof."

"It can't hurt. He should know so he can assign patrols to drive by and check from time to time."

"I need coffee."

She went to the refrigerator for milk, poured it into a cup and handed it to Judson when he followed her. It wasn't until she heard him talking to Brenna that she realized what she'd done.

"I can't believe I did that," she said when he returned.

"Did what?"

"Assumed you would take the cup to her. As if you're. . ."

"Her father," he finished.

He'd taken off his coat, and had his thumbs hooked on the front pockets of his jeans. His jaw was dark with a morning beard, and his hair looked like he'd just jumped out of bed. She'd never seen Timothy in such a disarray. Then again, Timothy would never have responded as quickly to a call for help as Judson had done.

"You know you're her first crush."

"It's the dog and the horse she loves."

"They don't hurt, but she's been fond of you since that first meeting."

"It goes both ways."

"She's not going to be happy with me if I sell the land and we move away from you."

He walked over and reached for her hands. "No decisions until after Christmas, remember?"

Chapter Seven

"IS THIS VAN'S WORK?" Avery studied the horseshoe reindeer. It would look so sweet beside her tree.

"Yeah, he makes them this time of year."

"I want it," she said, calculating how much she should bid for it in the raffle. "I'd really like two but I'll settle for one. This year."

"You could probably get him to make a couple of them for you."

Avery shifted and looked at Judson. "I hadn't thought of that."

They were at a Christmas carnival at the local elementary school. There were food and drink vendors and game booths, along with a long line of items being raffled off. All the proceeds from tonight were earmarked for new playground equipment.

For the past three days, she'd stayed at home, falling into the habit of leaving several lights on at night to make any intruder think she was awake. She made more candy cane shaped cookies–they were much more uniform the second time–wrapped presents and finished up her work on the national campaign project.

She had long telephone conversations with Judson each of those nights. After the calls ended, she had trouble sleeping, her thoughts tossing and turning along with her body. She liked the cabin Uncle Alex had left her, especially since she'd put her mark on the renovations. The quiet and the distance from neighbors enabled her to work uninterrupted or to relax and read for pleasure after Brenna went to bed. But she also admitted there were times she felt very isolated or hindered by the inconvenience of not being able to make a quick trip for groceries, or order in take-out if she wasn't in the mood to cook dinner.

So, when Judson asked if she and Brenna wanted to come

to the carnival, she'd been more than ready to get out of the house. Brenna, apparently had also been ready for some company other than her mother's—she'd pretty much run into the children's play area, supervised by high school senior volunteers.

"Wait! Are you suggesting I short-change the fund-raiser by paying Van outright for one of these?"

Judson's lips twitched. "No, I'm suggesting you bid on this one and then pay him to make you another."

Avery wrote a generous amount on the slip of paper and dropped it into the box. "Now . . ." She rubbed her hands together as she scanned the various booths. "Shall we play?"

"You chose."

She headed for the booth where the goal was to toss cotton snowballs into a bucket. Judson groaned when she beat him four snowballs to two. She then led them to water trough and they blew through straws to race plastic penguins. She beat him by a beak. At the wreath tossing, she snagged five of the cardboard trees while he managed a paltry one.

"That's it," he declared. "I'm picking something I can win."

While she laughed, he pulled her into the photo booth. "This is much better," he said, sitting her on his lap. Her laughter died as he held her head and kissed her.

She liked how he didn't rush to take the kiss deep. His lips touched hers, lingered, sweet and yet hinting at so much more. It was she who used the tip of her tongue to part his mouth, to touch and retreat playfully.

"Time's up," called someone outside of the curtain.

"I'll give you ten dollars for five more minutes," Judson said, his lips barely lifting from hers.

"You want pictures?"

Avery and Judson pulled apart, staring at one another. Then they began to laugh.

"Never mind," Judson said, standing and taking Avery's hand. He parted the curtain and they walked out. He dug into his pocket for a ten-dollar bill and handed it to the boy monitoring the booth.

"Let's get some hot chocolate."

"Coffee," Avery said when they stopped at a booth. "Oh, hello, Frances," she said, recognizing the girl.

"Frankie," she corrected, ignoring the snicker of the girl beside her.

"It's nice to see you again." Avery looked around to see which organization the sales would benefit. This one was for the local 4H club. "Uhm, is your father here tonight?"

"No."

"We'll have a coffee and a hot chocolate," Judson said.

"Sure. Cream or sugar?" she asked as she turned away to pour the coffee.

"Just black, thanks," Avery answered.

When she put the filled paper cups on the counter, she placed the coffee cup too close to the edge. It tipped over, forcing Avery to take a quick step back to avoid being splattered.

"Oh, I'm so sorry," Frankie said, without an ounce of apology in her voice. "I'll just get you another." She turned back to pour another cup of coffee.

Avery gripped Judson's arm, stopping him from saying anything. "Please, don't cause a scene. It's not worth it," she whispered.

"Here you go." Frankie offered the cup. "I hope it's not too strong."

"Just the way I like it." Avery hesitated. "Tell your father I said hello."

"Why did you say that?" Judson asked as they walked away.

"I don't want him to think I suspect him of anything."

"Avery," Mayor Scott called, cutting off any more conversation as she hurried their way. "I have a favor to ask."

"What do you need?" Avery asked, taking her first sip of the coffee. "Wow, Frankie wasn't kidding. This is strong coffee." She blew into the cup, cooling it enough for another swallow.

"We have the cookie decorating contest scheduled for next week. With you being new to town, I thought you'd be the perfect impartial judge."

"Well, I'm not much of a sweet eater."

"The contest is for the decorations, not taste, so no worries.

It's at six o'clock on the square. And don't worry about your little girl. We'll have someone keep an eye on her while you judge."

Avery drank more coffee as the mayor hurried off. "Why do I feel like I've just been run over by a bulldozer?"

"Everyone in town knows exactly what you mean."

Avery shifted to find two couples she recalled meeting at Audra's home at Thanksgiving. Pushing a stroller with their twin girls, Sydney and Ryland Evans wandered through the carnival. They ran Evergreen, a ranch for military families to reconnect after returning from deployment. The couple walking with them was Walker and Jessica Thorne. Avery set her coffee on the ground when she knelt in front of the stroller to speak to the little girls.

"Hello. Are you having fun tonight?" She smiled at the way the one on the left—Zoe, she thought—waved her rattle. Then she laughed when it flew out of her hand and knocked over her coffee.

"Oh, I'm so sorry," Sydney said, bending down to pull a cloth out of the diaper bag to mop up the liquid. "We'll get you another cup."

"No, it's okay." She handed the rattle back and stood, rubbing at the burn in her stomach. "This one's not sitting well."

The couples talked, keeping to gender lines with the men discussing ranching and the women talking about babies.

"You have nice friends," Avery said after the couples continued on.

"You keep forgetting, they're your friends too," Judson said.

"Do you think they're talking about us being together? And this?" She lifted the hand he continued to hold.

"Absolutely. Does it bother you?"

"No." She bit down on her bottom lip. "Does it bother you?"

"Avery." He stopped them in the center of the hallway, forcing people to walk around them.

"I told you, you're the first woman I've been interested in

since I returned to Burton Springs. And it has nothing to do with your land. It's you. I enjoy spending time with you. Why else would I allow you to con me into getting a Christmas tree?"

"You know you could easily put another tree in the kitchen."

He shook his head but his lips curved. "If I agreed to that, you'd think of another place to put one."

"Well, now that you mention it . . ."

"I didn't. You did."

She laughed, then bent at the waist with a gasp at the sudden sharp pain slicing through her stomach.

"Avery, what's wrong?"

"Hurt." She drew in a deep breath, only to take a step back . . . and violently empty her stomach.

IGNORING THE MESS, Judson swept Avery into his arms. People gasped, someone screamed. He kept his gaze on her, noted her features were pale enough for him to spot faint freckles on the bridge of her nose he'd never noticed. With relief, he saw Gabriella hurrying their way.

"Follow me," she said, leading him into the nurse's office. "Lay her down on that table." She opened drawers and pulled out a stethoscope. "What happened, Avery?"

"We were talking when I got this awful pain in my stomach. Before I could stop it, I threw up."

"What about before today? Have you been feeling okay? Has Brenna complained about feeling sick? Could you have caught a bug somewhere?"

"No, she hasn't said anything, and I haven't noticed her acting sick. We've stayed home the past three days."

She groaned when Gabriella pressed on her stomach. "You should step out, Judson."

"Why?"

"It's fine," Avery said. "Mostly I'm embarrassed I made such a mess."

"I imagine the mayor already has someone taking care of it. I have to ask." Gabriella looked up from Avery, to Judson, back to Avery. "Is there a chance you could be pregnant?"

"What?" Judson yelled.

"No," Avery answered quietly.

"Okay, what have you had to eat or drink while you've been here?"

"Just coffee."

Judson swore, and would have stormed out of the office if Avery hadn't caught his hand. "You said it tasted funny," he growled.

"I said it was strong. And bitter," she said, then rolled to her side and vomited again. "I'm sorry."

"Does your throat burn?" Avery nodded, and Judson thought the doctor looked a little pale. She walked to a small refrigerator and took out a bottle of water. "Drink this slowly, and only a little bit," she said. As Judson supported Avery while she sipped, Gabriella took out a tongue depressor and scooped a bit of the vomit into a paper cup.

"Tell me about the coffee," Gabriella said.

Judson related the details about Frankie spilling the coffee and then pouring a second cup.

"And she had her back turned to you while she poured the second cup?" He nodded. "Tell me what else was there. Around the area where the coffee was brewing."

Judson wasn't sure he could remember anything but the way he'd been looking at Avery. He'd been too angry over that stunt with the spilled coffee and had been struggling against the need to say something, causing the scene she'd asked him not to make. He should have known Daniel Gaines's daughter wouldn't let one failed attempt to make trouble keep her from trying another.

"You think she put something in the coffee?" Judson asked.

"I can't be sure, but there's no harm in treating Avery as if that's the case."

"Would it act so quickly?" Avery asked.

"It depends on how much of whatever it was, was added to the coffee. You said you haven't eaten, so your empty stomach didn't have anything to absorb or fight off whatever *may* have been put in the coffee. Plus, it had to be a small amount or you would have tasted it. So there's less chance of any damage." She patted Avery's shoulder. "Just lie here while I have Van take a look at the booth." She glanced at Judson. "He's just going to take a look."

"Sydney," Avery suddenly said, gripping his hand while she looked at Gabriella. "We were talking and one of the twins knocked over my coffee with her rattle. Sydney used a cloth to wipe up the spill." Her gaze pleaded with him. "You have to find them, warn them. I can't stand the thought of something happening to one of those girls."

"Van can do it." He pressed his lips to her forehead. "I'm not leaving you."

"I'll have Van find Sydney first. Between it and what I collected from the floor, maybe we'll get an idea of what made you so sick."

"Since we already know who," Judson said.

"Judson, we don't know for sure" Avery protested.

He stared at her wondering how she could be so calm. How could she doubt, when she was laying there pale and sick?

Gabriella paused with her hand on the doorknob. "I'll also alert the sheriff."

"I need to get Brenna."

Gabriella smiled for the first time. "I'll bring her to you."

Only it was the sheriff who walked in with Gabriella.

"Did you talk to Frances?" Judson asked.

"No, she'd already left. However," he said moving to block Judson from getting to the door. "Doctor Ferguson spotted some dishwashing liquid near the area where your coffee was poured. She's pretty sure that's what caused you to be sick, Avery."

"But you have no proof she added it to Avery's coffee, right?" Judson asked, wanting so badly to hit something.

"No," the sheriff said. "I can talk to her."

"Why bother?" He flexed his hand, frustrated that there was nothing he could do. "She'll deny having done anything wrong. Hell, she'll likely claim it was an accident."

They talked a little more, with Gabriella giving Avery a few basic instructions to rest, eat light meals and stay away from coffee for the next twenty-four hours.

"I just don't understand why she'd do something like that," Avery said after they'd arrived at her house. She'd settled Brenna in bed and now sat at the end of the sofa, her legs tucked under a quilted throw. She'd also taken a shower and Judson had brewed tea, trying, in vain, to not think of her wet and naked.

Now, he paced the room, straining with the need to do something more than brew tea or offer to heat up soup.

"She's Daniel's daughter. That's all the explanation I need."

And Judson had every intention of talking to Daniel Gaines about it. Not that he planned to let Avery know that.

He stopped in front of the lit Christmas tree. She had a mix of ornaments, including one of the Atlanta skyline, one with Brenna's baby footprint made to resemble a reindeer, and the falcon's crest logo he recognized from Londyn Fitzgerald's popular fantasy book series.

He pointed to it. "Are you a fan?" he asked.

"I have to be." She smiled when he looked at her. "Londyn was my college roommate. I designed the Falconer's Crest."

"No kidding? That's seriously amazing."

"She's trying to convince me to come to New York."

"For Christmas?"

"Yes." She set her tea down. "And to stay."

Conflicted by this news, Judson shoved his hands in the back pockets of his jeans and walked over to stare at the low simmering fire in the fireplace. If she went to New York for the holidays, it would put distance between Avery and Daniel. Selfishly, however, he wanted her to stay so he could spend time with her.

"I can't tell you I haven't considered it," she said. "Especially with everything that's been going on."

"You mean someone sabotaging your home and then trying to poison you?"

"We don't know for sure. There could have been something in the cup and she didn't notice it before she poured the coffee."

"How can you excuse her? How can you be so damned calm about this?" he exploded.

"Oh, I assure you, I'm anything but calm. How can I relax knowing someone wants to hurt me?" Her hands fisted on her lap. "Do you think I haven't considered whether or not it's worth the risk to Brenna to live where people value land more than life?"

Her face might be pale, but anger flashed brighter in her eyes than the glow of the firelight. He went over to her, knelt in front of the sofa, and eased her into his embrace. She trembled as her arms wrapped around his neck.

"I'm so damned pissed they're messing with my Christmas spirit."

His lips curved as he kissed her temple. "We can't have that now, can we?"

"I'm serious."

"I know. You're also worn out. You should go to bed." He stood, pulling her to stand. Then just held her close until he could feel her body relaxing. "Come on."

At the door to her bedroom, he again held her close. "I'll sleep on the sofa, just in case you need anything."

"Judson." She skimmed her lips over his throat. "You can sleep with me."

He was tempted, but knew he couldn't do it. When they became lovers, he wanted it to be because it was what they both wanted, when they wanted it. Not because she felt obligated and vulnerable. Her lips cruised along his jaw, in a slow pace that spoke of fatigue rather than seduction.

"No." He cupped her face, kissed her forehead, then gently pushed her back a step, closing the door on her . . .and the temptation she offered.

AVERY WOKE TO the sound of laughter. Not Brenna's toddler giggles but the deep-throated chuckles of a man. Why was Judson here so early? That was when she remembered the events of the night before.

At first, she'd been more mystified than furious at the idea that Frances Gaines might have doctored her coffee. It just didn't make sense. She'd had two short interactions with the girl and while Frances hadn't been friendly, Avery had dismissed that as usual teenager behavior. Besides, it was her father who wanted her land, not Frances.

"Come back here."

Avery jumped at the harsh whisper, then grinned when Judson chased Brenna into her room.

"Mama."

"Good morning, baby." She pulled her gaze away from Judson, wincing a little at the way her head spun.

"I've got her," Judson said before Avery could lift her.

"'Udson," Brenna said, pointing when he placed her on the bed.

"Yes, I see." She looked up. "Has she been awake long?"

"About an hour."

"I'm sorry."

"We had fun." He sat beside her legs, drilling a fingertip in Brenna's belly.

"Ho. Ho. Ho," Brenna laughed.

Avery blinked, then looked over at Judson.

"It's easier for her to say than Santa," he explained.

There was something very intimate about the three of them sitting on her bed in the early morning. Judson's hair was tousled, his shirttail pulled from the waist of his jeans. Avery closed her eyes against the wave of longing that hit her. What would it be like if this was a normal morning?

"Are you okay?"

"Fine." She opened her eyes. "Probably better than you feel after sleeping on the sofa."

"It's not much different from catching sleep while waiting for a mare to foal."

"Oh? Try being the one in labor. For twenty-six hours." When he winced, she ran a hand down Brenna's hair. "All I remember is that incredible rush of love I felt when I held her for the first time."

Suddenly Judson was off the bed and walking away. "Someone's here."

"'Udson," Brenna called, scrambling off the bed and chasing after him.

When Avery reached the great room, she discovered Judson holding Brenna in his arms, scowling out the window. "It's Daniel." Turning to her, he caught her running a hand through her hair.

"I'll get it," she said at the knock on the door. "Daniel, good morning," She stepped back to allow him inside. He carried a bouquet of red roses. "You'll have to excuse my appearance. I slept late this morning."

"I don't blame you." He stopped, giving Judson a curt nod. "These are for you," he said, handing her the roses. "I was so sorry to hear about you being sick last night. The sheriff spoke with Frances. While she admitted she'd spilled the first cup of coffee, she assured both of us that she would never do anything to hurt someone."

Judson swore under his breath, loud enough that Brenna repeated the oath. "No, Brenna," Avery said. "That's a bad word."

"'Udson said."

"Yes, and he was bad to say it. Judson slept on the sofa last night," she said to Daniel. "In case I had another reaction."

"Why don't I take those flowers and put them in water for you." Judson juggled Brenna and reached for the flowers. His fingers tightened, just for an instant, against hers.

Daniel watched him disappear and then faced Avery. "Again, I'm so sorry about what happened last night." His smile troubled her more than his frown of disapproval at Brenna. "I hope this little misunderstanding won't prevent us from spending time together."

Avery might have doubts that Frances had deliberately tried to harm her, but she couldn't believe the audacity of this man to brush it aside so easily. Calling on skills she'd watched her ex-husband employ, she kept her voice neutral.

"I'm sure you'll understand that I'm not making any plans until I feel a little steadier on my feet. And I haven't found a dependable babysitter for Brenna."

"Of course. If there is anything I can do in the meantime to speed along your recovery, don't hesitate to call."

"Thank you again for the flowers."

"Avery . . ." He glanced toward the kitchen, then back at her. "I hope you know I say this because I'm worried about you. Are you sure you can trust Ford?"

"Judson?"

"Don't get me wrong. He's well-liked around here. But, well, are you aware that he made an offer for your land through his attorney?"

"I know my attorney received an offer. He didn't mention a name."

"That's what I mean. Why would he try to keep his offer a secret? Then there's the trouble you've had since moving here. Have you considered Judson had someone cause it so he could come to your rescue? After all, a snake doesn't bite until he's close enough to be sure he hits his target." He took her hand. "Please be careful."

"I will. Thank you for your concern. And the roses."

Avery waited until he drove away before she went into the kitchen. All her annoyance faded beneath the pleasure of finding Brenna standing on a chair, biting down on her bottom lip as she broke an egg against the side of a bowl. A good bit of it spilled down the outside of the bowl, but Judson patted her arm and said, "Good job."

"What's going on here?"

"Mama. I make breakfast." She frowned. "You go bed."

"Breakfast in bed?" she guessed, spotting the toast waiting on a plate.

Judson handed Brenna a fork, showing her how to beat the egg mixture. As she did, he offered Avery a cup of tea while staying close enough to the chair to make sure Brenna didn't fall off.

"You heard him?"

"I heard," Judson said before repeating his earlier oath, this time low enough that Brenna didn't hear. "You told him Harley didn't give you the name of the person who made an offer for your land."

"He didn't. You told me." She sipped her tea. "And isn't it interesting that Daniel didn't admit he wants the land, too?"

"Mama, go bed."

"You're right, sweetie. I don't want to spoil any more of this morning." She pressed a kiss to the top of Brenna's head. Then, she leaned over and kissed Judson. "Don't burn my eggs," she teased.

ON A FACETIME call later that afternoon, Londyn frowned after Avery related what had happened at the carnival. "Your life is beginning to sound like the plot of a bad book."

"How would you know? You only write good ones," Avery answered.

"I don't know about good, but the one I was working on is finished."

"Your book? Oh, Londyn, that's great. Wait—" She narrowed her eyes. "Why don't you look happy about it?"

"I'm processing," she said with a shrug. "Since it's the last one in the series, it feels kind of like saying good-bye to a family member." She laughed, but there a sliver of sadness in the attempt at humor. "Whoops. Did that already."

Being a pastor's kid, Londyn had been held to a higher standard by her father. Invariably, she'd displeased him in one way or another. When her first book had been published, and reached all the best-seller lists, her father had expressed disappointment rather than pride. In all the years Avery had known Londyn, not once had her friend had any contact with her parents or her younger brother and sister.

"I really wish you'd come out here," Avery said. "The change of scenery would be good for you. Brenna was asking about you just yesterday."

"No fair using that sweet girl to lure me. Besides, you could always come here."

"I can't, Londyn. Not this close to Christmas. Brenna is so

excited. She's loving all the Christmas events we've been to in town."

Londyn braced her arm on the table and cradled her cheek in the palm of her hand. "That may be, but are you sure you're safe?"

"I'm being careful."

"And this cowboy? Judson? You trust him?"

"Enough that I'm going to sleep with him."

Londyn sat up. "Seriously?"

"It's what I want."

"Hey, I'm not judging." Avery knew she wouldn't. Londyn had grown up under the smothering veil of constant scrutiny. "I just want you to be happy."

"It's what I want for you too." Londyn looked away from the screen. "What's going on, Londyn?" Avery asked. "You haven't been yourself since before I moved to Montana."

"I'm fine," she said, too quickly to sound convincing. "There're a few things with work I need to handle. Don't worry."

"That's impossible." She heard Londyn sniff, something that worried her even more. In all the years they'd known one another, not once had Avery ever seen Londyn cry. "Will you let me know if there's anything I can do to help?"

"Who else would I call?" She looked back at the screen, her eyes over-bright. "Promise me you'll be careful."

"I will if you will."

Chapter Eight

FOR THE NEXT three days, Avery kept a light schedule where her work was concerned. She really had little choice, since new friends kept stopping by at random times to chat or bring her food. Gabriella had come both as a friend and a doctor, not only checking on her health but also delivering the horseshoe reindeer her bid at the carnival had won.

On the evening Judson was coming by to drive them to town for the cookie decorating contest, Avery studied her reflection in the full-length mirror as Brenna played with plastic horses on the floor beside her. She'd considered a dress, but decided it wasn't practical in this weather. Instead, she wore knee-high boots with black leggings and a green sweater.

Still, she was as nervous as a young girl about to go out on her first date.

"It's silly," she said to Brenna. "I'm just going to look at cookies."

"Cookies," Brenna repeated, abandoning her toys and running toward the kitchen.

"My own fault." Grabbing her phone off the bed, she followed her daughter. She ended up having to change Brenna's outfit but considered herself lucky at avoiding cookie handprints all over her leggings. She was repining the bow in Brenna's hair when she heard the knock on the back door.

"'Udson," Brenna called out.

"Judson," Avery corrected. "Come in," she called out, setting Brenna down and letting her run to him.

"Well, who have we here?" he said. Avery pictured him sitting on the bench, lifting Brenna onto his lap. "Now don't you look pretty. Have you been a good girl?"

"Good," Brenna repeated.

"I'm glad to hear that. Where's your mama? We don't want the mayor mad at us for being late."

"Right here," she said, stepping around the corner just as Brenna called for her.

Avery had the very feminine pleasure of watching his eyes flicker over her, go dark, and then take another unhurried look. Starting at the toes of her boots, he looked up her legs, pausing a half second before skimming her stomach and breasts and finally locking gazes with her.

"On the other hand," he said, standing and walking her way with Brenna in his arms. "We could forget about the cookie contest all together and stay home."

"Cookies," Brenna said, squirming to get down.

"Now you've done it. No." Avery tore her gaze away from Judson and tapped a fingertip on her daughter's pouting mouth. "No more."

"She had some already?" Judson asked.

"Right before you arrived."

"That doesn't seem fair. If she had a treat, I should have one too." His eyes twinkling with seductive mischief, he leaned forward to kiss her. "Give her another," he said, his mouth hovering over hers. "So, I don't feel guilty for being greedy."

This time, he did more than simply kiss her. He parted her lips, using more force than he had before, and tangled his tongue with hers. There was a carnal hunger to this kiss that stirred an answering hunger in her.

She lost all sense of time and place. All she knew, all she wanted, was for Judson to continue kissing her, to continue stoking this fire he'd lit within her.

"Kiss."

Brenna's joyful exclamation succeeded where common sense had failed. Avery and Judson broke apart and stared at one another. Lips swollen by pressure and need curved in twin smiles.

"Well, she's not wrong," Judson said.

"We should go." Avery stepped around him so she could get her coat. But she heard his low whisper.

"While we still can."

It felt natural to give him the keys to her SUV while she buckled Brenna in the car seat. He shook his head in amusement when Christmas music played through the speakers.

"Don't even think of touching that dial," she warned as she reached for her seat belt.

"I wouldn't dare."

"And drop that Scrooge attitude. Especially since I know it's all an act."

"I have you to thank for that."

"Thank or blame? I was just teasing," she said when he shifted to stare at her.

"It's different—Christmas I mean—when you can share it with someone who adds to the excitement."

Touched by his words, she leaned over the console and kissed his cheek. "I know I've never enjoyed a Christmas as much as I'm enjoying this one."

"Then I guess we'd better get to town."

"Yes." She sat back and smiled to herself. Some decisions were made regardless of time, some were made impulsively, others made after a great deal of thought. And some choices were easy and right. She'd made hers, and it filled her with an anticipation that was bigger than the excitement of Christmas morning. "There's a lot to celebrate tonight."

They were on the outskirts of town when Judson's cell phone rang.

"'Ondyn," Brenna called out from the back seat.

"No," Avery said. "That's Judson's phone. You can answer it," she told him with a smile. "I promise not to listen."

He hesitated, then pushed the answer button. "Yes?" In the dim light of the car's interior, it was hard to make out his expression but his voice clearly announced impatience. "It has to be subtle, not obvious." He listened, then shook his head before saying, "No, not that. Okay," he said after another brief pause. "That could work. Do it." Saying nothing more, he ended the call, and a few minutes later, they arrived in town.

Once again, the town was full of people, Christmas music

and activities. When Avery noticed a crowd, she walked over to discover the town had set up a temporary skating rink. The string of overhead lights reflected off the ice like diamonds.

"Looks like the mayor convinced the town to go through with another of her ideas," Judson said. "Tonight won't be the last favor she asks of you. Don't say I didn't warn you."

"She's a force that can't be ignored, isn't she?"

With Brenna settled in the designated play area, they headed for the tent where a dozen tables were set up, each with two displays. Avery muffled a groan.

"What's the matter?" Judson asked. "Too much Christmas?"

"Please. There is no such thing as too much Christmas."

"If anyone would know, it would be you." He leaned forward to whisper in her ear, "If I'm a good boy, do I get something extra under my tree?"

She looked at him, thought of all the flirty teasing that had been such a part of their phone calls the past few nights. Not caring who took notice, she rose on her toes and kissed him. "What if I like my men to be bad?" she asked. Then, before he could say anything, she walked away.

After declaring a cookie-decorating winner, Avery lingered, talking with the contestants, accepting a box filled with samples from each display. The tent would now be opened to everyone, the cookies sold and profits earmarked to buy books for the school library. She made a mental note to ask Londyn if she'd be interested in donating a set of her books.

She sat beside Judson as he drove a wagon full of carolers through the city streets. While she enjoyed the music, and the sense of community, she kept an eye out for Daniel and his daughter. Later as they drove home, Judson took them through a couple of neighborhoods so Brenna could see the way people decorated their houses.

"Now she's going to be asking me for more lights," Avery commented as they drove down the long, dark road to her house.

"I can string some up outside your place, if you want."

"No, what we have inside is enough for this year."

"Bye 'Udson," Brenna said as he passed the sleepy girl into Avery's arms after she unlocked the back door.

Avery's heart squeezed at the way he kissed her cheek. "Sweet dreams, sweetie."

She caught his hand and kissed his cheek. "Come inside. Stay."

Wordlessly, he followed her, silently helping her with coats, gloves, and hats. Then he quietly waited for her by her tree while she put Brenna to bed.

Her heart swelled when she found him staring at her Christmas tree. From the glow of lights, she glimpsed an expression of longing on his face that was impossible to miss. Not for the tree, the decorations, or the scatter of presents, but for everything the tree represented—the hopes and dreams it stood for.

Going over to him, she wrapped her arms around his waist and pressed her body against his back. His hands covered hers.

"You know how much I love Christmas."

"Kind of hard not to," he managed with a strained laugh that delighted her.

"It's not that I'm naïve. Or that I'm only pretending, for Brenna's sake." She rose on her toes, kissed the side of his neck. "It would have been easy to become resentful after caring so many years for an ungrateful father. Then, there was the bitterness of the divorce. Instead, I choose to believe in magic—the magic of the season."

She slid around so she could face him. "Will you come to my bed and make some magic with me?" Then she took his hand, and led him to her room.

He hovered in the doorway, taking in the unfolded covers and candles she'd lit after putting Brenna to bed.

"Do you mind?"

He turned to close the door behind him. "I'm not stupid, so no." He crossed the room and took her face in his hands. His eyes were intent, filled with a promise that sent a ripple of excitement down her spine. "But fair warning—some of that magic we share tonight is going to be dark and demanding."

What woman wouldn't be thrilled to hear that level of desire in the man about to become her lover? "Show me."

He kissed her softly, sweetly, even as his hand slipped under her sweater. She shivered at the scrape of his rancher's hands, then arched her back when he cupped her breasts through the silk of her bra. She tugged his shirt free and made quick work of the buttons before pushing it off his shoulders. Breaking the kiss, she traced a fingertip down the thin line of hair that bisected his chest.

"Avery," he groaned, pressing his forehead to hers when she moved her fingertip to the button on his jeans before dipping, ever so slightly beneath the waistband.

She let her hands roam over him, enjoying the solid strength of his muscles, the flat plane of his stomach, the delicate quivers of excitement her touch provoked. But she wanted more.

Stepping back, she pulled her sweater over her head, then reached behind her for the clasp of her bra. His hands brushed hers away.

"Let me."

She shivered slightly when he dropped the bra to the floor and the heat of his gaze touched her naked breasts. Then the warmth of his mouth enveloped her as he suckled, while the firm hold of his hands at her waist kept her anchored. Sensations bombarded her, leaving her almost crying with the need for him to go further, do more. Harder. Faster.

He knelt as his mouth trailed open-mouth kisses down to her stomach. Then he tugged her slacks and panties down, leaving them at the tops of her boots, but giving him the access he sought.

She cried out his name with the first touch of his tongue at her core. His hands molded around her rear, holding her while he took his time bringing her close to the peak, then drawing back before she could experience the thrilling ride of release. Then he put her through the same erotic rise-and-fall, over and over . . . until finally, he let her crest.

Urgency gained the upper hand as they stripped, caressed and explored. There were no secrets, no desire unfulfilled as they rolled over the bed. Greed slowly, beautifully, gave way to sharing. When he finally protected them and slipped inside her, there was no outside world, no doubts, or concerns.

Together they accepted the priceless magic of trust.

Afterward, Judson held her close, her head pillowed on his shoulder, their legs entwined. This, too, was part of the magic of this night, a kind of intimacy she'd always craved but had never experienced.

She felt none of the awkward insecurity of not knowing what to do or say. She could lay here, warm and satisfied, and a little drowsy, with her lover doing the same.

"This is nice," he finally said. "I don't usually stay long after." He kissed her. "But I'd like to stay the night if it's okay."

"I'd like that."

"Should I open the door in case Brenna calls for you?"

"No." She arched when his hand cupped her breast. "The monitor is on."

"Can she hear us?"

Her laugh turned into a moan when his hand traveled lower and began to stroke her. "No," she managed to say.

"Then let's make some noise."

AVERY WOKE THE next morning in the best way possible— in Judson's arms. Their night together had been incredible. He'd been demanding, but so had she. Curled against his side, with his arm stretched over her waist, his body felt solid and warm beneath the covers. She'd like nothing better than to stay like this a little longer. However, her mother's internal alarm clock was counting down the minutes before Brenna woke.

Her attempt to ease away and out of bed was met with the firm resistance of his arm. "Too early."

Her brows rose when he shifted and his morning erection pressed against her hip. "Not when you have a three-year-old."

"Do you want me to leave before she wakes up?"

She didn't regret inviting him into her bed. But she also hadn't thought through what it would mean to Brenna if she found him here. She turned to face him. "I'd love to spend the morning in bed with you, but I think it will be less confusing for her if you aren't here."

"I understand."

Only when he started to draw away, when she missed the feel of his body against hers, she pulled him back in her embrace. He lifted a brow in confusion.

"We have time."

There was just enough time to savor the pleasure of touching and kissing, of exploring. Their lovemaking was hurried, but no less satisfying than it had been last night.

"I'll make you some coffee before you leave," she whispered into the quiet contentment that followed.

"Appreciate it."

There was no awkwardness as they dressed, had their coffee, then made plans for her and Brenna to come to his house and decorate that day, and enjoyed a long kiss good-bye. The tension started when Judson stepped onto the back porch.

"You've got to be kidding me."

"What?" Avery followed him outside, only to find him kneeling by his truck. His tires had been slashed. A quick look confirmed her tires had received the same treatment.

"I'll call the sheriff," she said.

"Wait." He walked to her. "Let's go back inside so you don't freeze." In the foyer, he took off his hat but not his coat. "Avery, do you really want the sheriff to come out here?"

"Judson, our vehicles were vandalized. He should know someone was here."

"Maybe, but he'll know I spent the night here."

"You can't possibly think he'll suspect you of doing this?" she asked a second before his meaning became clear. "Oh. You don't want him to know you were with me."

"That's not it." He reached for her, a hint of frustration in his gaze when she stepped back. "I'm trying to protect you, damn it."

"By hiding what happened?"

"By taking care of you and your vehicle without alerting the person who did this. I can call my father." He used his arm to swipe at what looked like nervous sweat above his top lip.

"Hodge can pick up some new tires and exchange them for the damaged ones."

Avery shivered, suddenly recalling Daniel mentioning that Judson always seemed to be the one who rescued her. He'd been the one who found the leaking water faucet and the electricity breaker that had been shut off. He'd been the one who'd suggested that Frances Gaines had done something to Avery's coffee. With growing dread, she recalled part of Judson's telephone conversation in the car last night.

Subtle. Not obvious. Do it.

"Mama."

Avery turned on her heel and dashed off to Brenna's room. Her thoughts swirled with questions. She couldn't imagine Judson doing what Daniel had suggested. Surely what she'd overheard on that telephone conversation was just a coincidence. It couldn't have anything to do with what they'd just discovered.

Only her subconscious taunted her with reminders of how wrong she'd been about her ex-husband.

"No," she whispered, refusing to believe Judson would resort to such behavior when he'd been upfront about offering to buy her land. If anything, it made her even more suspicious of Daniel, who'd put the idea into her mind. He had a reputation for being ruthless about getting what he wanted. Hadn't she been warned by several others about him?

"Good morning, sunshine," she said to Brenna, who stood in the middle of her bed. She knew she wasn't allowed to climb down unless Avery was in the room. "Did you have sweet dreams?"

"Hungy."

"Okay."

In the kitchen, she saw no sign of Judson. Once she had Brenna settled at the table, she peeked out the window. Steam puffed out of the tailpipe of his truck, indicating he sat inside with the engine, and heater, running—honoring her request that Brenna not see him this morning.

"I was wrong. Stay here," she said to Brenna before heading for the back door. Opening it she waved a hand to catch his attention. "Come inside," she shouted when he rolled down the window.

"I'm fine. It's the tires, not the engine that's ruined."

"Come inside." Leaving the door open, she returned to the kitchen and poured two cups of coffee.

"'Udson," Brenna called out when he came into the kitchen. "Doggie?"

"Sorry." He chuckled. "Not this morning. Thanks," he said when Avery handed him a cup. He'd removed his coat, hat, and boots. His hair was mussed and he clearly needed a shave. She recalled the feel of his coarse hair on her skin as he'd kissed her with focused intimacy.

"I called the sheriff. He's on his way."

A breath that was lodged in her chest broke loose as her suspicions eased.

"I'm not embarrassed that we spent the night together, Judson."

"If you think I am, then you don't know me very well."

"But we haven't known each other all that long, have we? And the reason we met is because you were hoping to convince me to sell my land."

He looked away and shoved his hands in his front pockets. When he looked back at her, his eyes were troubled and his mouth formed a tight line.

"All done?" she asked, lifting Brenna from the chair. "Why don't you go play while Judson and I talk?"

"'Udson play."

"Not right now." He knelt to her level. "Why don't you get some blocks so we can build something." He stood as she ran off.

Avery looked him in the eye. Her daughter had trusted him from their first meeting. She had trusted him with her body. It was time to trust that he would give her the truth.

"Please forgive me for asking this, but I have to know . . . Did you not want me to call the sheriff because you paid someone to slash the tires?"

Chapter Nine

HIS EYES WERE dark against the skin that drained of color. "Why would you ask...? Wait! It was Gaines, wasn't it? He suggested I did all these things so you'd trust me."

"I've been betrayed by one man who told me what I wanted to hear." She held up a hand. "You know how that feels."

"I do, and that's why I would never lie to you." He pulled his phone out of his back pocket, cued up the screen and handed it to her. "That phone call last night? I hired someone I know to install a security system, with cameras, for your house." He pointed to the call listing. "I wasn't going to tell you until after it was in place so you couldn't argue with me about it."

"You want it to be subtle, not obvious."

"Well, yeah, so whoever's behind this won't know they're being filmed."

She set the phone on the table, then took his face in her hands and kissed him. "Thank you."

"I wasn't home when my mother died in a house fire. I will always wonder if Melanie would have still gone for a run if I hadn't left the apartment. Trust me when I say there's nothing I won't do to keep you and Brenna safe."

When the sheriff arrived, he asked questions, took photos, wrote a report for their insurance. Right before he left, Hodge drove up, delighting Brenna by bringing Ginger along, with two sets of tires in the back of his truck. While Judson and Hodge exchanged the tires, the sheriff sat at her kitchen table with a cup of coffee.

"Now, there's a happy sight," he said, gesturing the cup in the direction of where Brenna and Ginger played tug-of-war with an old kitchen towel.

"I'm surprised she hasn't asked for a pet of her own." She

rubbed her temple. "I just don't think I can handle training a dog right now."

"I'm sorry there isn't more I can do for you, Ms. McClain,"

"Avery."

He nodded, still watching Brenna and Ginger. "Judson told me about the security system." Now he looked at her. "Have you given any thought to staying in town."

"Yes, I have, but this is home—*my* home. And I'm not going to let someone chase me away."

"I'll have patrols start making rounds out this way."

"You haven't been doing that already?"

"No."

"Oh, I thought... After someone tampered with the electric breaker, Judson said he would ask you to have patrols come by."

"I'll check with a couple of the deputies, but I don't remember seeing the request." He stood, then nodded. "I'll see myself out. You be careful."

A little later, Brenna was predictably upset when Judson and Hodge left, taking Ginger with them. Avery turned down Judson's whispered invitation to come to his house, explaining that she wanted to finish up all her work before Christmas. Besides, she wanted to be home during the security installation he'd told her would begin the next day.

Later that night, after Brenna was asleep, she put in a couple of hours extra work. Realizing it was nearly midnight, she double checked all the windows and doors before getting ready for bed. She'd just settled beneath the covers when her phone chimed.

"It's not too late to call, is it?" Judson asked.

"No."

"What are you doing?"

"I just came to bed."

"I wish I was there with you."

She ran her free hand over the space where he'd slept last night. "What are you doing?"

"Staring at this sad-looking Christmas tree."

She smiled. "It's going to be beautiful by the time I finish with it."

"Are you going to used that silver string stuff?"

"Tinsel? I wasn't planning on it. Unless you want it."

"No. I hate that stuff."

"Have you decided on your topper?"

"Topper?"

She laughed and snuggled into her pillow a little more. "Never mind. I'll think of something."

"You sound tired, Avery."

"It's been a long day." She hummed low in her throat, remembering, yearning. "After a long night."

"I have a feeling this one will be long for me, too. Just not for a good reason. Sleep well, Avery. Keep your phone close by."

"I will."

She ended the call and, wishing she held him rather than the phone, fell asleep.

IT TOOK JUDSON'S friend, Ed, two days to install the security system and hide the cameras. Mostly because he was a friendly sort who liked to take long breaks while he enjoyed Avery's invitation to have coffee and Christmas cookies. Since he had a dog with him—an aging beagle—he also allowed himself to be entertained whenever Avery took Brenna outside to play with the dog.

"I'm going to have to seriously consider getting her a pet," she told Ed during one of those play times. "That is, if I stay here."

"I know someone who has a boxer close to dropping her litter." He chuckled as he pulled wires through a faceplate just inside the back door. "Her female got a little too friendly with a shepherd that came nosing around her backyard."

By the end of the second day, he'd completed the installlation and walked her through how to operate it. She gave him credit, along with a nice tip, for the fact that the cameras were virtually impossible to spot, yet they provided multiple views of the yard and house.

The next day, after packing a few things and heading to Judson's house, Avery felt comfortable enough with her winter driving skills that she called Londyn on the way over.

"'Ondyn," Brenna said from the back seat. "Hi."

"Hello, sweetie. When are you going to come see me?"

"Going see 'Udson. Doggie. Horsie."

"I see I've lost my top billing," Londyn said.

"She misses you," Avery said. "If you came out here, you'd be on top again."

"I don't think so. But I'm glad to hear you got the security system." There was a brief pause. "I got one myself."

"Why? Londyn, tell me what's going on. And don't give me that bull that everything is fine."

"Mama?" Avery looked at her daughter's frown. "You mad at 'Ondyn?"

"No, sweetie. I'm not mad at Londyn." She stopped shortly after turning onto the road leading to Judson's house. Putting the car in park, she reached into the basket, pulled out a yogurt pouch and handed it back to Brenna. "Now," she said into the phone after disconnecting it from the handsfree option. "Tell me what's happening."

"I've just been getting some emails from a fan who's not happy that I'm not writing anymore Falconer's Crest books."

"What kind of emails? Threatening?"

"No. They're more pleading. This guy is telling me that the Falconer's Crest world is like family to him. Kind of ironic, don't you think? I lost my family because I wrote these books."

"Your family is narrowminded and have never deserved you. What does the publisher say? Never mind. I'm sure they're trying to use it as leverage to change your mind since they aren't in favor of you discontinuing the series in the first place."

"Done, Mama."

Avery took the empty pouch from Brenna. "I don't like the sound of this, Londyn."

"Well, I don't like worrying about someone slashing your car tires or trying to poison you."

"Go, Mama. See doggie."

Londyn's chuckle came through the phone. "Yes, mama. Not to mention seeing your hot cowboy. And that's another reason I'm not coming out there. No way am I being a third wheel."

Avery began driving again. "Maybe you'd find a strong cowboy of your own."

"I've got enough trouble to deal with."

"I don't like knowing you're alone."

"I've always been alone."

"Well, gee . . ." Avery said after she swallowed down sympathy for the loneliness in her friend's voice. "Thanks so much."

"You know—"

"Lights, Mama. Lights," Brenna interrupted, clapping her hands.

"Oh, Londyn," Avery whispered. "Judson's put lights around the barn door," she said, watching as he added lights along the roof edge. Standing below, tracking his progress, Hodge watched. A quick look confirmed lights already lined the roof of the house. A wreath hung in the center of every window.

"Then you'd better take Brenna out of the car to enjoy them," Londyn said softly. "Be careful, Avery."

Not sure if her friend's warning was for the trouble she'd dealt with or about her relationship with Judson, Avery promised she would, then climbed out of her SUV.

"Are you saving any lights for the tree?" she called out.

"I put them on before I started out here," he called back, continuing to belly crawl along the roof. "Go in and see. This won't take much longer."

"'Lights, 'Udson," Brenna called out.

"You bet," he answered.

"I like lights."

"There's more inside."

"Mama, go."

Letting Brenna tug her along, Avery stepped into the mudroom and sighed in relief at the warmth chasing away the outside cold. Since she hadn't seen Ginger outside, she took off Brenna's coat and let her run off in search of the dog. Happy laughter and barking echoed through the house. At ease, she carried her bags into the great room.

The big tree glittered with white lights. Off to one side were boxes that, she discovered, held white and silver ball ornaments of various sizes. In another box she found bows of red and green plaid. In yet another, she came across red battery-operated candles, a pillow printed with an image of a horse-drawn carriage in the snow, a nutcracker, a ceramic snowman figurine, a plush Santa Claus, and a small, exquisite wooden Nativity.

"For someone who claimed he wasn't into Christmas," she mused, thinking of him outside stringing a mile of lights on the rooftop. "He isn't holding back."

It was tempting to start decorating, but she wanted to share the experience with Judson. Besides, there was no hurry.

They had all night.

JUDSON STOMPED the snow off his boots before stepping into the mudroom. He'd hoped to be done with the outside lights before Avery and Brenna arrived. For a moment he stilled, absorbing the sensation of knowing the house wasn't empty. It was more than the coats hanging next to the empty hook where his would soon hang, more than the discarded boots. It wasn't the scent of something simmering on the stove, even as his stomach rumbled, or the sound of Christmas music that chased away the loneliness that so often welcomed him.

It was the knowledge that *they* were here, waiting for him.

It hadn't been easy for him to stay away from her the past couple of days. And not because he was worried, although of course that was part of his need to be with her. He'd enjoyed their nightly phone calls, but he wanted to hold her.

He drew up sharp as he approached the great room, standing still to take in the picture before him. Avery sat cross-legged on the floor, staring up at the Christmas tree. In a simple white sweater and jeans, with feet covered in socks lined with candy canes, she looked beautiful and peaceful in the glow of the lights. When she was here, his home felt warmer—a place for friends and family to gather.

More than decorations, it was her presence that made his house feel like a home; more than gifts, it was the thought she put into everything she did; more than the promise of cookies, it was the time she would spend baking them.

Somehow this woman had brought hope and joy into his life, and he couldn't see that fading when the Christmas season ended.

As if she sensed him, she turned her head in his direction and smiled.

It took all his willpower to resist going over to her, laying her back and making love to her right then and there. Again, not just tonight, but always.

"'Udson."

The startling realization of his feelings faded as Brenna ran to him, her arms raised so he could pick her up. Here, too, was something he wanted beyond the holidays. Saying nothing, he carried Brenna over to one of the boxes. "Have you been good?" he asked her as he knelt, balancing her on one thigh. She nodded, and he pulled out a short strand of lights. Flicking on the switch on the small battery box, he gave them to her. "Now you have some lights of your own."

"My lights, Mama."

"Yes, I see. Tell Judson thank you."

She kissed his cheek before sliding off his leg and carrying the lights over to the basket of toys. Judson looked over to see tears in Avery's eyes.

"It's okay, isn't it? The lights?" He frowned. "I didn't think about if she might trip or wrap them around her neck."

"She'll be fine. I'll only let her have them when someone is around to keep watch."

Crossing the room slowly, he sat beside her. They moved together, each leaning forward, until their mouths met in a tender kiss. She brought a hand to his cheek, her thumb stroking the rough texture of his afternoon shadow before she slid her hand to the curve of his shoulder, where her fingers massaged muscles stiff from hanging the lights. Unable to resist, he slipped a hand under her sweater and used his thumb to rub at her hardened nipple through the lace of her bra.

"Maybe I should keep the tree up all year," he whispered.

Her lips curved as she kissed him. "Then it would become ordinary." She leaned back to look at him, her eyes lit by the inner fire their kissing had started. "Not magical."

"No day with you would ever be ordinary."

She lowered her forehead to his chest. "Are you implying I'm a challenge?"

"Yes."

"I like that."

"I like that you didn't start decorating the tree."

"It was tempting." She met his gaze. "I wanted us to do it together."

"Will you stay tonight?"

"I brought a bag, just in case you asked." She smiled, and leaned forward to kiss him again. "I'll be right back." When she rose in one fluid move, he watched her as she walked to the kitchen. Curious about what she was up to, he almost followed, but her words about supervising Brenna when she played with lights ran through his mind.

He started a fire, then pulled the Christmas pillow out of the box and tossed it onto the sofa. Avery returned, carrying a tray with cheese and crackers along with two glasses of white wine and a short cup with a spill-proof lid.

"Supper won't be ready for another hour or so." She set the tray on the coffee table and offered him a glass, then touched hers to his. "To making Christmas memories."

"Where do you want to start?"

The slow curve of her lips and the wicked gleam in her eye had him thinking of ways to make memories that had nothing to do with decorating a tree.

"I peeked in the boxes earlier," she said, taking another sip of her wine. "We'll start with the ornaments."

"I'll take the red, you hang the silver."

"Your engineering degree is rearing its ugly head," she teased. "We can't be that regimented. We have to mix them up, by color and size, as we hang them."

"And the plaid bows?"

"No, they go on last."

"So, there are procedures."

"Plans," she corrected, in a way that left Judson wondering if they were still talking about the tree.

"Show me."

"Gladly."

She knelt by the box, pulling out all the boxes of ornaments. "First we take them out of the storage boxes," she instructed, handing one to him. "And put all the ornaments into the big box. Where are the ornament hangers?"

He blinked. "Ornament hangers?"

"Yes, the little wire things that fit through this loop." She pointed at the top of an ornament. "And the other end hangs on the tree branch."

"I guess they're necessary?"

She laughed, hard enough to have Ginger and Brenna coming over to investigate. "Oh, Judson, really?" She plopped down on her very fine butt and wrapped an arm around her waist. "You didn't order them?"

"I thought they came with the ornaments."

He scowled at her, which led to her laughing again. He walked over to the coffee table to take a slice of cheese and put it on a cracker. He offered the first one to Brenna, then put together another snack and stuffed it in his mouth before he said something to ruin the evening.

"Okay," she said, once she quit laughing. "We can figure out something. Have you got any ribbon?"

"Why would I?"

"String. Surely you have some kind of string that will work."

"There's some in the barn."

"Not rope. It has to be thin enough to fit through this loop."

"I can figure that out." He helped himself to more cheese and crackers. "I guess I'll have to go back out in the cold and look for some."

"Why don't we come with you?" She nodded in the direction of the big window. "It's getting dark enough for the lights to show. We can decorate after supper, when Brenna's asleep."

HE WAS ADORABLE. Avery had to keep her tongue tucked into the side of her cheek to keep from laughing as he grumbled about going outside to look for string. She knew he was putting on a show for them, trying to cover embarrassment for his oversight.

Bundled in coats, hats, and boots, they stepped outside. The sun was lowering on the horizon, and the big sky above glowed a reddish orange. Snow on the ground enveloped them in a layer of quiet. The lights he'd strung on the barn and house were a pale glow, waiting for the sun to disappear so they could shine bright and clear.

"It's so beautiful," Avery whispered.

"I like the view from inside better."

"No, you don't." She reached down for a handful of snow, molding it into a ball.

"Don't start something you're not prepared to finish."

"My thoughts exactly," she said. With a smile, she winged the snowball toward the barn. It fell yards short. As they walked the pathway, Ginger ran ahead, sniffing and taking care of business.

"I like that you used white lights inside and outside."

"That way I don't have to keep them separated when I pack them up."

Inside the barn, Judson found a ball of string right away, then took Brenna around to pet some of the horses.

"Sorry." They all turned to see Hodge standing at the rear door to the barn. "I heard something and thought I should check on the horses."

"We needed some string," Avery said when Judson and Hodge exchanged head nods. "How are you?"

"Fine."

"Would you like to join us for supper?"

"It's nice of you to ask . . ." He looked at Judson before he shoved his hands in his front pockets. "But I'm working on something."

"I'll box up a meal for you. Judson can bring it over to you."

"Thanks."

Back outside, they spent a frigid five minutes admiring the lights and letting Brenna make and throw her first snowball before they returned to the warmth of the house.

Avery removed her hat and ran her fingers through her hair. "I hope you don't mind that I invited Hodge to supper."

"It's fine. I'll take him something later. Right now, though, I'll cut the string into six-inch lengths and put them on the ornaments." Hanging up his coat, he left the mudroom.

"Well," she said to Brenna. "It looks as if we might get another Christmas miracle."

She gave him space and time by staying in the kitchen, setting the table in the dining room, taking frozen biscuits out to bake. At one point, Judson brought the tray of cheese and crackers, along with a glass of wine, to the kitchen. Before she could say anything, he gave her a hungry kiss, then went back to the great room.

"Keep that up—" Avery said later, as Judson served himself a third helping of potatoes, "—and there'll be nothing left to pack up for Hodge."

He grinned. "I'll make sure to tell him it was good."

He offered to do dishes but she insisted he'd be more help entertaining Brenna. When she'd cared for her father, chores like this always depressed her. Now, she realized the difference. Her father had eaten what she'd cooked, but he'd had no taste for the food, or appreciation for her efforts. He'd eaten because he'd had no choice.

Judson, on the other hand, enjoyed the food she prepared. She liked the sense of comfort she felt in his house, knowing he didn't find fault with everything she did. She liked hearing the low tones of his voice as he teased and played with her daughter.

Hurrying through the rest of the clean-up, she joined them in the great room. "Ready to start decorating?"

"Get your phone," Judson said, lifting Brenna and guiding

her tiny hand to hang the first red ornament. Avery blinked back tears as she framed them in. "Send me a copy, will you?" Once she had, she stopped him from setting Brenna down. "Hold on," she said, and went to one of the bags she'd brought along.

"Traditionally, this is the last to be put in place, but I think we can make an exception." She offered a star she'd cut out of cardboard.

"Yellow," Brenna said. "I color for 'Udson."

"You said you didn't have a topper," she said when he stared at it. "I know it's homemade, but you can't have a tree without something at the top. Once you find something you like better, you can just toss this."

"That's not going to happen."

"Wait." Avery lifted the camera and took a shot of Judson and Brenna placing the cardboard star at the top of the tree.

"Now your turn," he said, exchanging the phone for Brenna. "I figure you didn't get any when you decorated your tree."

"I did it at night so she woke up the surprise of the tree." They hung three balls before Brenna lost interest and wanted to play with the basket of toys.

While Judson hung the ornaments, Avery positioned the plaid bows. With the last one in place, Judson wrapped his arms around her waist, holding her against his chest as they looked at the tree.

"This is crazy."

"What do you mean?" Avery angled her face so she could see him.

"I'm standing here, looking at this tree that's only got ornaments on the front half."

"It makes the tree look fuller since the back is against the wall. No one will know but you and me."

"They will if I have a party."

"What?" Avery spun around to face him. "Seriously?"

"I told you it was crazy. But I figured that I should start to give back a little. I've lived here for a while now, and have been invited to other people's homes more times than I can count. Maybe it's time I opened up mine."

"It's a wonderful idea."

"I'm already getting a headache."

She rose on her toes to kiss him. "I'll help."

"Oh, no. You're the one who started this snowball rolling. You handle the details, all of them."

"But . . ."

"I trust you."

He drew her close and she settled her head on his chest, then looked up and pulled away. "Oh, sweetie," she whispered when she noticed Brenna nodding off where she sat next to Ginger. She went over to her daughter, then picked her up and looked at Judson. "I didn't think about whether or not you'd have a bed she could use."

"I'll show you the guest room." Upstairs, he led her into a spacious room with a queen-size mattress covered with an ivory spread beside a single nightstand. "I haven't done anything with the other two bedrooms yet," he said, standing by while she changed Brenna into pajamas and tucked her in.

Her heart warmed when Judson motioned for Ginger to leap on the bed. "Stay," he said then reached for her bag as they walked out. "Master's at the back of the house."

This bedroom was twice the size of the first one. A king-size bed with an intricately scrolled ironwork headboard that she guessed was Van's work, was covered with a navy spread. On the right side of the room, a love seat and overstuffed chair with an ottoman fronted the wide windows that provided a spectacular view of the night sky. She wondered what Judson would say if she suggested a small Christmas tree in the corner.

"The bathroom?" she asked, gesturing toward a partially closed door. He nodded. "Would you mind if I freshen up a bit? I won't take long." She walked over to kiss him. "I'd like another glass of wine if you don't mind." Not waiting for an answer, she took her bag from him and headed for the bathroom.

It wasn't nerves that had her rushing through changing into the pale blue nightgown she'd brought. Anticipation heightened her need to be with him. Remembering what they'd already shared filled her with an eagerness to know more, do more.

When she came downstairs, she was thrilled to see the room lit only by the fireplace and the lights on the tree.

"You read my mind," she said, taking a drink from the glass of wine he offered.

"Every night when we talked on the phone, I imagined you here." He shook his head. "My imagination was nowhere close to how amazing you look tonight."

She felt a rush of power at the way he stared at her, his eyes dark with desire. "When you open your house to friends and celebrate the magic of Christmas . . ." She smiled a little as she pulled the string at the neckline of her gown, gave a little shrug, and felt the silk slide off as it dropped to the floor. "I want you to remember tonight."

Together, they sank to the floor beneath the glow of the Christmas tree lights. They moved slowly, gently, taking time to caress and savor. Avery felt the abrasion, deliciously erotic, of his jeans and flannel shirt against her bare skin. His hands stroked her, held her as his mouth explored and tantalized. She'd set out to seduce him, but she was the one who arched and asked for more.

Her first thrilling release was soon followed by a second before he finally stripped. She welcomed his weight as he eased inside her, as their bodies found the fit that perfectly suited them. Their gazes held as their bodies moved, as the connection they'd found deepened, before giving way to the fever that overwhelmed them.

Chapter Ten

JUDSON STOOD, his hands shoved in his back pockets, and watched Avery drive away.

"Everything okay?"

Judson jumped a little, surprised he hadn't caught the scent of his father coming close. Maybe the old man had really given up smoking. Just another way Avery had impacted his life.

"Fine."

"Never known you to have a woman stay."

Heading toward the barn, Judson fought the discomfort of his father mentioning his love life. "Keeping an eye on me?"

"Used to be, I'd be outside and see you come and go."

"Used to be?"

"Twelve days ain't a lot, but it's a start."

"You should check with Gabriella. They have those patch things that are supposed to make it easier."

"I started it on my own. I'll finish it on my own."

Judson stopped and stared at his father. Maybe a muscle ticked at his jaw, but his color looked better, his eyes were clearer, and so far, he hadn't coughed once. After so many years of being chained to a habit, it couldn't be easy to shake off the craving.

"I'm proud of you."

Hodge blinked and it made Judson uncomfortable to realize he'd never thought that before, let alone said the words. Maybe he still blamed Hodge's smoking for his mother's death, but he knew his parents had loved one another. Maybe his father hadn't had as successful a ranch as Judson was on his way to establishing, but Hodge also hadn't had his wife's life insurance money to give him a start. He thought again of Avery, and how she'd come all this way to start a new chapter in her life. Maybe he and his father had been at odds more often than not, but there was no reason that couldn't change.

"I could use some help with a project I have in mind for one of the upstairs bedrooms, if you have the time."

Hodge nodded. "I've got plenty of time."

Hours later, Judson sat in front of the lit Christmas tree. He missed Avery with a physical ache but his thoughts were more than sexual.

Even with a fire going in the fireplace, the room felt cold. He'd eaten a cold sandwich standing at the kitchen sink instead of sitting at the dining room table with a meal someone had taken the time to make. The basket of toys waited in a corner instead of turned upside down, its contents left all over the floor by a curious little girl. Ginger lay still, turned toward the back door as if waiting for it to open. The tree wasn't nearly as inviting as it had been when Avery stood beside him, her face lighting up after he suggested the party. It felt as if everywhere he looked, there was a reminder of the night they'd had together.

Throughout the afternoon, he and his father had worked upstairs, mostly in silence but there had been moments when they'd talked about good times in the past. As if understanding Judson's conflicting thoughts about the future, Hodge didn't comment on the bed frame they were building. If he had asked, Judson had intended to pass it off as simply something good to have on hand. But it was thoughts of what else would be good to have that tantalized his thoughts.

He'd lived in this house, alone, for several years. While it had often felt empty, it had never felt as lonely as it did now.

AVERY LOOKED AT the stocking. It wasn't the same as the cable knit ones she had hanging over her fireplace. But did it matter? She wasn't sure what to do, but then Brenna decided for her. The little girl reached for the display. "Mine."

"No," Avery corrected. "Ours are white stockings with our names embroidered in red. This stocking is red, so it would need to be embroidered in white." She rubbed her nose against Brenna's. "Do you think he'll notice?" She thought of those hazel eyes that could look so intently at her, almost into her very core. "Of course, he will."

She added a few more items to her growing pile before she realized she was putting off the true reason she'd come to town today.

After her day at Judson's two days ago, she'd been more optimistic about staying in Burton Springs. For both of their benefits, she knew she should find an early childhood program for Brenna. She'd read about one that was held in the church, and decided to check it out.

Ten minutes after she'd entered the director's office, she came back outside, dazed by the unexpected invitation for Brenna to stay.

"Are you frozen in place?"

Avery blinked, realized that somehow she'd made her way down the street and had stopped in front of Tammy's Diner. The thick bundle of her coat, boots and a scarf couldn't disguise Rhonda Johnston's innate sensuality.

"I'm a terrible mother."

"I'm no expert, but I'd have to argue that point. At least I would, if we were somewhere other than standing on the street in the dead of winter. Come with me." Grabbing Avery's arm, she opened the door.

The bell chimed as they walked inside and the warmth and scent of coffee and fried food welcomed them. Christmas music provided a backdrop to conversation and kitchen sounds coming from the pass-thru window behind the main counter.

As was her way, Tammy appeared at their booth, pouring coffee before they could remove their coats.

"You two been Christmas shopping?"

"Yes. No," Avery answered, earning a lifted eyebrow from Tammy. "I just left Brenna at a pre-school class."

"Oh, honey." Tammy rubbed a hand over her shoulder. "Did she cry when you left?"

"No. She was so busy playing, she didn't even notice." Avery had regained enough composure that she saw the confusing look exchange between Tammy and Rhonda. "I'm feeling guilty because I'm thrilled to have a couple of hours to myself."

"You're too smart for that," Rhonda said as Tammy walked away, pausing by a nearby table to refill cups. "You work hard and have a successful business; you deserve some time for yourself."

"How do you know I have a successful business?"

"I sleep with the local sheriff. He checks out everyone who moves into his town."

"He looked into my background."

"It's his job."

"And he told you."

"A little."

Avery waved a hand between them. "Is this your way of gathering more?"

"When I first came to town, I went out one night with Daniel. It was just dinner, but there was no spark. I don't waste my time if there's nothing of interest to keep me coming back." Her red lips went straight and firm, her eyes took on a distant fire. "He thought otherwise. I know how to take care of myself," Rhonda assured her when Avery reached for her hand. "A week later, I came outside to find every window in my car had been smashed. There was no proof then either." She smiled over the rim of her cup.

"On the other hand, maybe I should thank him. That little stunt led me to the sheriff's office. And I'm happy to say, there was, and still is, plenty of spark there," Rhonda said with a grin.

"I just don't understand why he'd take this approach for a piece of land. Didn't he consider that I might be less likely to sell to him because of these incidents."

"Because it's about more than the land. Men like Daniel don't take well to the word 'no', and they definitely don't like coming in second place to another man. You call me, anytime, if there's no one around to help you."

As Rhonda glanced out the big window, her lips curved. "Although, if it was me, that would be my first call," she purred.

Avery looked over and spotted Judson leaving Harley Barker's office. More than a spark swept through her at the thought of being with him.

"How much time did you say you have without your little girl?"

"Enough," Avery answered.

With Rhonda's low chuckle following her, she reached for her coat and hurried out of the diner.

"Hey," Judson said when he spotted her. "I didn't know you were coming into town today." He took her coat and held it out for her. "You shouldn't be out here without this on."

"I left Brenna at the childcare program. For two hours. Well, closer to an hour and a half now since I was just having coffee with Rhonda."

She inched closer, then rose on her toes and nipped his ear. "Is there somewhere close by where we can go?" Oblivious to the fact that were standing on the street corner, she skimmed her lips down his jaw.

Shoving her coat into her hands, he drew out his cell phone. "Hey, Doc. Is that apartment above the clinic empty? Can I use it for an hour?" He hissed out a quick breath when Avery, behind the curtain of the coat she held, skimmed her hand over the swell of his jeans. "No, nothing's wrong. I just need somewhere to spend some time." He grinned. "Yeah, I bet you do. Thanks, I owe you."

He ended the call as he grabbed her hand and they all but ran down the street. People paused to watch them, but Avery didn't care.

"Do I want to know how you know about this apartment?" she asked, pressing against his back as he fought to unlock the door.

"Gabriella lived here before she married Van." He looked over his shoulder. "I think she guessed the real reason I wanted the code to the door."

"I don't care."

He shoved the door open, pulled her inside the downstairs foyer, only to turn her so she was backed up against the door. His hands tossed her coat to the floor, found their way under her sweater so he could cup her breasts. Her legs sagged.

"Oh, no." He held her up, his thumbs flicking over the hard nubs of her nipples through her bra. "You started this. Don't wimp out on me now."

"Judson." She practically panted his name. "I've never wanted anyone the way I want you." She shoved at his coat. As it fell to the floor, she began unbuttoning his flannel shirt, gave up halfway and opened the zipper on his jeans. "God, now. Here."

"Wait."

"No." Her blood pounded with a primal beat that begged for relief. She freed him, wrapped a hand around his firm warmth.

They wrestled together to remove clothes, allowing him to intimately stroke her until she was all but screaming for more. Finally, he thrust inside her.

It was fast. It was consuming. It was glorious.

Holding onto him, trying to catch her breath, she had to admit to herself that she'd fallen in love with Judson.

It wasn't just the amazing sex. It was the kindness in how he cared for his father, despite their past differences. It was the friendships he took time to nurture, his commitment to the community. It was how he went out of his way to do the little things, like arranging for the security system for her home or putting up lights for Brenna, that made it impossible to not love him.

"Hey." He tried to nudge her face up, but she continued to hide in the crook of his shoulder. "Avery, did I hurt you?"

"Again." What stormed through her wasn't just sex but she'd used it to avoid blurting out what she couldn't yet say. Her mouth took his in a frantic kiss. "Take me to a bed, Judson. I want you again." She continued to torment his mouth, his jaw, his throat, as he carried her up the stairs.

There, she wasn't able to hide behind speed. But with every touch, he took a firmer grip on her heart. She wondered how he couldn't feel the difference when each touch, each caress, each kiss, seemed to hold so much more than it ever had before.

The climax was slow and beautiful, spreading brightness along with the thrill, especially since it was one they shared.

Afterwards, wrapped in his arms and snuggled against his side, Avery resolved to be content. She wouldn't expect more than the happiness she felt right now. Later, hopefully much later, she might have to deal with disappointment and heartache if they went their separate ways. But for right now, she shut her mind to the future and soaked up the contentment of the present.

"Is everything okay?" she asked.

"I'm in bed in the middle of the day with a sexy woman. What could be wrong?"

Her lips curved and her heart skipped as she kissed his chest. "I meant because you were coming out of Harley's office."

The pause was so short, she almost missed it. She would have if she hadn't been pressed so close to his side that she felt him hold his breath for an instant.

"No problems. Just some paperwork I needed to sign." He rolled over and nestled between her legs. "Lucky for me, I came to town when I did."

She lost count of the times he kept her on the brink of a climax, trembling with need and the hint of the glory she knew he could give her. All she knew was when he finally took her over that edge, her heart, body, and soul were his.

Later, they picked up Brenna, and walked around town, stopping to admire the window decorations and listen to the elementary school choir sing Christmas carols.

"No way," Judson said when they were nearly run down by a pack of boys rushing by, carrying sleds under their arms. "Come on," He grabbed her hand. "I didn't know they were doing it this year."

"Doing what?"

"Sledding. Here." He handed her Brenna when they reached the bottom of a hill, rubbing his hands in boyish anticipation that matched the grin on his face.

"Okay boys," he said, handing over bills for the sled he'd selected. "Time for the master to show you how's it done."

She grinned when he whooped with delight as he took the first ride down the hill. No sooner had he reached the bottom, than he popped up and ran back to the top. He rode with a fearless grace—probably the same way he sat on a horse. Juggling Brenna, she reached into her coat pocket and drew out her phone.

"I can hold her."

Avery looked over and felt a quick flash of embarrassment when she saw Gabriella, who had to have figured out why Judson had asked for use of her apartment. Still, she handed Brenna over. Who better to trust than a doctor. Besides, she wanted to capture the joy on Judson's face.

She zoomed in the camera as much as possible, clicked on the image of him settling belly-flat on the sled at the top of the hill. His quick grin told her he'd exchanged trash talk with the teenager beside him. Shifting to the video feature, she followed him down the hill. Her heart stilled, then leapt along with him as he aimed for a dip that sent him airborne for one quick instant. His laughter rang out as clear as the cold night.

"That was great," he said after he returned the sled and rejoined them.

"Your body is probably not going to think so tomorrow morning," Gabriella said.

"Worth it."

"The best things usually are." Gabriella rubbed her cheek against the top of Brenna's head. "Call me if you have anything more than the expected aches and pain."

They talked a little longer until Gabriella noticed Avery shivering. Handing Brenna back, she told them to get out of the cold night air, then she walked away to do the same.

Strings of twinkling lights along the street made it easy to find their way to where Avery had parked her car. She started the engine to warm the interior while Judson belted Brenna into her car seat.

"She's half asleep already," he said.

"Come home with us."

He grinned with the same enthusiasm as he had on the sledding hill. "I thought you'd never ask." He kissed her. "I'll be right behind you."

THE NEXT MORNING Avery waved as Judson drove away, just as the sun peeked over the horizon. They'd enjoyed a quiet evening cuddling on the sofa while watching a movie before going to bed. Then they'd fallen asleep, holding onto one another.

It said something, she believed, that they reached for one another even when sex wasn't involved. Before Judson, Avery hadn't realized how much she craved the casual touches that increased the sense of intimacy between two people.

The sound of her cell phone had her running to the bedroom. "Hello," she answered, frowning when there was nothing but silence.

Assuming it was a spam call, she was just about to disconnect when an indistinct voice warned, "You need to leave."

At the click, she searched the recent call list to find this one listed as *Unknown caller*.

Switching to the app for the security system, she scrolled through video of the night before, but saw only her and Breanna and Judson arriving back home, then Judson leaving this morning. Her first instinct was to call Judson, then she considered calling the sheriff. However, as was the case with all the other incidents, she had no proof of who was behind it.

Suspicion, and a nagging sense of trepidation stayed with her throughout the morning. But before long, her anger grew stronger than worry. How dare someone threaten her in her own home? Then she remembered that they'd already done that several times already. So why wouldn't they continue? And, perhaps, do more damage?

Later that afternoon, after Brenna's nap, she drove into town. Her first stop was the clinic.

"Hello," Gabriella said when she entered the reception area from the back rooms. Her professional gaze scanned Brenna's face. "Is someone not feeling well?"

"No, she's fine. We're both fine."

"But something's wrong." She gestured to the play area off to one side. "She can play while we talk if you want. We can sit over here."

They settled on hard plastic chairs separated by a small table displaying a variety of magazines and medical pamphlets.

"I'm surprised you're not busy."

"I'm expecting Mr. James to come by shortly for his physical and flu shot." Gabriella's smile dimmed a little, and Avery assumed it had something to do with the health of her patient. "Did you want to make an appointment?"

"No, I wanted to talk to you about the apartment. The one above the clinic. Will you rent it to me?"

"But your house?"

"I imagine you've heard that I've had some problems at my house." Gabriella nodded. "I just thought I should have somewhere to go. Just in case."

"Avery, has something happened?"

"No." She sighed in defeat as Gabriella simply stared at her. "I received a strange phone call this morning. It came in as an unknown caller so there's no way to trace it. But it worried me."

"I'm sure it did." Gabriella took Avery's hand. "Did you tell Judson? Or the sheriff?" When Avery shook her head, she asked, "Why not?"

"There's nothing either one of them can do. Please, Gabriella, don't mention it. I just want to have an option if I feel the need to get away."

"You wouldn't go to Judson's?"

"I don't want him to feel obligated."

"Obligation would not be his reason for asking you to stay with him." Gabriella chuckled as Avery's cheeks flooded with heat. "Listen, I understand how you're feeling, but I'm going to encourage you to tell him. So, no, I won't rent you the apartment. It's open for you whenever you want."

After thanking Gabriella, Avery left the clinic, and stopped by Fresh Touch Interiors to finalize details with Kathy Davis for Judson's party. On the way back to her car, a display in the window of Buds and Blossoms tempted her to duck inside and make an impulsive purchase. Then she decided to take the long way home. It was past time she checked out the boundary of her property.

Spotting the stream, with a cluster of trees on the other side, she recalled fishing and swimming in this place when she visited Uncle Alex. "If we're still here in the spring," she said to Brenna, "we'll come back and spend the day exploring. If it's not too cold, you can splash in the shallow part of the stream. And maybe I'll try my luck at catching some fish for our supper."

"Snack, mama."

"Alright. Let me find a good place to stop. I don't want to get stuck and have to call someone to tow me out." She drove further, following the road as it topped a hill before it spanned the stream and fronted a large area. She swung the car around so she could retrace her path before she stopped and reached into the basket she kept in the passenger floorboard.

"Here you go," she said, opening the bag of cheese crackers before stretching an arm over the seat to give them to Brenna. Turning back to the basket, she pulled out a juice box.

"Horsie," Brenna called out.

Less than six feet from the passenger window, sitting on a horse with a rifle across her lap, was Frances Gaines.

She looked older, with a hat pulled low on her brow, and was wrapped in a heavy coat. With a barely noticeable kick of her heels, she had the horse going around the hood of Avery's car and coming to a stop beside the driver's window. Defiant, Avery pushed the straw into the juice box and handed it to Brenna before she lowered her window.

"You're on Golden G land."

"We were just out for a ride. I didn't realize I'd crossed the property line."

"Horsie," Brenna called again. A quick look in the rearview showed her reaching out her arm.

"There are signs posted."

"I didn't see any."

"Are you calling me a liar?"

"No. I'm saying I didn't come onto your property for any reason other than to turn my car around. Look, it's your father who wants my land, not the other way around."

"My father likes you."

As if she realized how much she'd revealed by that one statement, Frances reined the horse to turn around. "Stay off the Golden G," she said before riding away.

"Horsie," Brenna cried.

"Home," Avery said.

Chapter Eleven

"ARE YOU SURE you want to do this?"

"Absolutely. It's always been one of my Christmas fantasies."

"Well." Judson winked. "Who am I to deny you a fantasy?"

Avery looked away, her cheeks turning pink. God, it turned him on at how she could be so seductive and energetic in bed, but still blush at the tiniest bit of flirting. It was just one more facet of her personality that appealed to him.

"I'll have my cell phone if you need anything," she told Hodge, who stood by holding Brenna. Judson didn't have the heart to tell her that the service wasn't dependable where they were going.

"His mama had more of a hand raising him than I did," Hodge said with a nod toward Judson. "But I think I can handle an hour or two with this one."

It had been three days since Avery and Brenna had been to the ranch.

During that time, Judson and Hodge had kept busy finishing the bookcase headboard they'd added to the bed Brenna had used at their last visit. Brenna hadn't given it much attention—she'd been more interested in chasing after Ginger—but Avery had tears in her eyes as she thanked them both when she saw it.

"Okay, but don't let her talk you into more than one shot of tequila," Avery teased. "I don't want her to have a hangover the next morning." While Hodge hooted with laughter, Judson took her hand and helped her up to the wagon seat.

"It's not like we haven't done this already," he said once he was beside her and had flicked the reins to urge the horses.

"That was around town, with other people in the wagon behind us." He'd enjoyed having her sit beside him. Now, she straightened the heavy wool blanket over both their legs. "This is just us."

He could have argued they could find a better, warmer, way to spend time together, but he had to admit it was a good day for a ride through the countryside. A fresh inch of snow had fallen last night, with no wind and a weak sun keeping the temperature comfortable. Getting in the mood, he switched on the sound system and *Silver Bells* rang out.

"Besides, we need some mistletoe for the party." She nudged his shoulder. "To hang in a dark corner."

"You keep going like this and we're not going to have any new Christmas traditions left."

She turned to him, and for an instant he thought he caught a flicker of something sad in her gaze. "Maybe they won't be new, but that doesn't mean they can't become traditions."

"I tried every year to convince my mother to let me open a gift, just one present, on Christmas Eve," he said.

"Why on earth would you do that? You only have to wait one more morning. Besides, anticipation is half the fun."

"Sometimes," he said.

"Were your gifts from Santa wrapped? I keep going back and forth about what to do with Brenna's."

"I'm surprised." She looked at him, her brow lifted. "For someone who is so crazy about Christmas, don't you know Santa's gifts are always wrapped," he continued. "Tearing off the paper is half the fun."

"I would have guessed you'd be the type to rip off the wrapping in a rush rather than being slow and careful."

"Depends on what I'm unwrapping."

"Which will be nothing while we're out here in the cold."

"It could be another new Christmas tradition."

She snorted, then gasped. Judson tugged on the reins, bringing the wagon to a rolling stop. Following her line of vision, he spotted the white-tailed buck.

"Oh, it's beautiful," she whispered.

"A six-pointer," he said, referring to the antler size. "It's unusual for one to be out and about this time of day."

"Maybe he's playing hide and seek." She turned to him, grinning. "You know, the reindeer games Rudolph wasn't allowed to play."

He grinned back at her, then shook his head and flicked the reins to get the horses moving again. The deer ran off in the direction of the woods.

"How do you know where you're going? Where your property ends?"

"I have a short stone wall at two of the corners. Eight-foot-tall posts are at the other two."

"They'd be easy to spot then."

"That's the point. What are you getting at, Avery?"

"Returning from town the other day, I decided to take a drive along my property line. I was telling Brenna about fishing in the stream with Uncle Alex and how, maybe if we're still here in the spring, we'd come back and she could splash in the cold water. She was more interested in having one of the snacks I keep in the car. I didn't want to risk getting stuck in the snow or mud so I drove a little further, looking for a spot wide enough that I could turn my car around."

He frowned when he noticed her hands were clutching and releasing the blanket. Saying nothing, he brought the horses to a stop.

"I had reached over the back seat to hand the snack to Brenna, when she suddenly yelled '*horsie*'. When I looked up, Frances Gaines was sitting on a horse in front of us." Avery swallowed. "She had a rifle across her lap."

He couldn't swear, could barely breathe. But every nerve inside him trembled with the knowledge of what might have happened.

"Did she point the rifle at you? Or Brenna?"

"No. But she told me that I had crossed onto Golden G property, that there were signs posted. I apologized but then my temper got the best of me." Avery looked at him. "She said her father likes me, something she did not sound happy about, before she warned me to stay off their land. And then she left."

"And you haven't had any trouble at the house?" he asked,

knowing she hadn't since he'd had Ed install her security app on his phone. He didn't view it as his right, even if he'd paid for the security, nor did he see it as an intrusion on her privacy, though he thought she might. He saw it as one more way to protect her.

"No."

He frowned at her quick answer. "Avery, what happened?"

"He sent me flowers. A plant, a poinsettia, for the holidays. Judson . . ." She grabbed his arm when he flicked the reins. "You can't do anything."

"Want to bet?"

"It will only make the situation worse."

"Do you think I'm going to stand aside, knowing you and Brenna might be in danger?" He had to do something to burn off the anger that suddenly filled him. And the fear. Wrapping the reins around the brake lever, he jumped off the wagon, stalking away and staring into the distance.

"I want to ask you to stay at the ranch," he said. "But I know you won't."

"I can't."

He swung around. "No, don't get down. Your feet will freeze in those boots."

"I thought you said they were fine?"

Since they were the knee-high boots she'd worn before, it was easy to smile. "Avery, I dream of you in those boots. And nothing else." It was easier to laugh when color flooded her cheeks. Climbing back onto the wagon seat, he cupped her face and kissed her. Somehow, he'd figure out the best way to protect her. Just because she wouldn't agree to moving in with him didn't mean he wouldn't try to convince her to stay with him as often as possible.

"Are you sure we need that mistletoe?" he asked as his lips skimmed hers.

"Yes."

"Okay." He flicked the reins as he winked at her. "After we get home, we'll figure out which corner is best."

"I AIN'T NO SCROOGE, but I also ain't no Santa Claus,"

Jacob Reece said, his voice as rough as his seventy-year-old, weathered face. "Damn it, Judson. I like your operation and I think this breeding will be good for both of us."

"I want this deal as much as you. I just need a little more time to try and acquire the extra land. If you give me until the first of the year, that'll still give us plenty of time for spring breeding."

"First of the year," Jacob agreed, hanging up without another word.

Judson rubbed a hand at the back of his neck. He meant what he'd said to Jacob—he did believe the breeding operation would benefit both of their ranches. The extra pasture land was as important to their plan as selecting the best stallion and mare to breed. Judson had spent the last two days searching for alternatives to Avery's land. And the last two nights wishing she was beside him.

"I was just thinking about you," he said when he answered his vibrating phone.

"We're fine. There's no reason for you to come," she said, as if she could see him already heading for the mudroom for his boots.

"What happened?"

"A hunter spotted a small fire on the, uhm, northeast boundary of my property. He was able to put it out on his own, but he called the sheriff and told him about it. I wanted to make sure you didn't hear about it from anyone else. We're fine. I promise. The fire was nowhere near the house."

He sat down on the bench, rubbing Ginger's head when she rested it on his leg. "The northeast boundary is not far from where your land butts up against Daniel's."

"Yes, I know. The sheriff said it could have been left behind by another hunter who was careless."

His reply to that was a short, succent, oath. He hated the thought of Daniel watching them. "Damn it, Avery, just sell me the damn land and then he'll leave you alone."

"I will not be bullied into selling my land," she said, softly, cooly. "By anyone."

"Don't compare me to him."

"What else can I do when you're both after the same thing? God, it's times like this that I start to wonder if Uncle Alex actually did me a favor when he left me the land and cabin. Maybe I would have been better off just selling it in the first place and moving somewhere else."

His throat burned with the thought that he might never have met her. "You might have been better off, but I wouldn't be."

"You'd have the land."

"Yes, but without you being here, I wouldn't have a Christmas tree, wouldn't have enough lights strung along the roof that my house can be seen from space." He lowered his voice to a whisper. "I wouldn't be looking forward to hosting a Christmas party with you by my side."

"I have a confession," she whispered after enough time had passed to make him question if he'd said too much.

"Yeah?"

"I bought some new lingerie."

"We're cancelling the party. No way am I standing around, playing nice with friends while images of you in something black and lacy run through my head."

"It's red. Christmas red."

He groaned, a harsh sound that echoed. "Avery, you're killing me."

"I've never done that to a man before." She paused. "I like it."

He liked that they'd gotten past the tension of a few seconds earlier. He liked that they'd recaptured their easy flirting that always held the hint of a promise. And more than anything, he liked that while she second-guessed coming to Burton Springs, she didn't say anything about leaving.

"I KNEW THIS LACK of Christmas spirit was just a coverup," Avery said as she and Judson, with Brenna on his shoulders, walked through the downtown Festival of Trees display. Each tree, available for purchase, had been decorated by a group or business in various themes, most keeping to Christmas topics, but a few used the opportunity to promote. She grinned at the one sponsored by Fresh Touch Interiors, impressed with the way they'd used miniature hammer and saws, sprinkled between doll furniture. She took pictures, planning to send them to the mayor. The City of Burton Springs website could use a makeover. With any luck, the photos might entice the city to consider her taking over as webmistress.

"I have no idea what you're talking about." Judson said.

"Uh, uh." She bit down on her bottom lip as she held up her phone. "Who is it that I have photos of, sitting on Santa's lap?"

"I just did that so Brenna wouldn't be afraid."

"Sure, just like you bought her that lighted candy cane she's holding."

"Light, Mama," Brenna obligingly chimed in while waving the plastic candy cane, almost knocking herself in the head.

"And I guess I'm the reason why you bought the tree decorated with hearts and ribbons."

"Well . . ." He winked. "You did say you thought the sitting area of the master bedroom could use a tree." He leaned over to kiss her. "I like the idea of making love to you by Christmas lights."

The cold weather had no chance against the warmth that rose within her.

"Here's a sight to warm the heart on a cold night," Gabriella said as she and Van approached.

The doctor's cheeks were rosy, her eyes bright as she held her arm tucked through her husband's much larger one.

"Hey," Judson said. "I thought you were going to Chicago?"

"Tomorrow," Van answered.

"We're taking a trip down memory lane before we go home and finish packing. It felt like the right thing to do," Gabriella said, her voice thick with her accent. "I really hate that we'll miss your party."

"You need the rest," Van said.

"While I can get it." She kissed his cheek before she looked at Avery. "I haven't seen you around town since last week."

"No," Avery said, understanding Gabriella was asking if she'd had any more trouble. "There hasn't been a need."

"You didn't mention being in town last week," Judson said.

"I, uhm, well, it's Christmas. I can't tell you all my secrets."

Gabriella smiled as she looked up at Brenna. "Don't you look festive tonight?"

"Lights," Brenna said, waving the plastic candy cane. "Ho. Ho. Ho."

"Soon," Judson reminded her. "Hey, watch the hat," he said when she hit the brim with the candy cane. In one smooth move, he swung her off his shoulders and settled her at his hip.

"You're so easy with her," Van said.

"She makes it easy." Judson ran his fingers over her thigh, freeing a giggle.

Avery watched Van and Gabriella exchange an unspoken decision. Van lifted their joined hands before kissing the ring circling her finger. Then, clearing his throat, he looked at Judson.

"Maybe you can give me a few hints."

If Avery had any lingering doubts about loving Judson, they vanished as soon as his face lit up with joy. Before she could reach for Brenna, he handed her over. He stepped forward and cupped Gabriella's face. "Everything okay?"

"Perfect."

He kissed her cheeks. "You make sure you keep it that way."

"Should I remind you I am a doctor, Judson? I believe I know what to do."

Then he turned to Van and engulfed the bigger man in a back-slapping embrace. "What is it about you two and making declarations here in the middle of town?"

"You caught us at the right moment," Gabriella said, swiping away a single tear. "We hadn't planned on telling anyone until after we see my *famiglia*."

"Then you'd better go. Knowing Mayor Scott, she'd sniff out the hormones and broadcast your news to everyone."

Gabriella laughed. "You're not wrong. Merry Christmas, Judson, Avery." She kissed both their cheeks, then Brenna's. "I hope Santa brings you many toys."

"Lights," Brenna declared, making all the adults laugh.

"That's so great," Judson said, again settling Brenna on his shoulders once Gabriella and Van walked away.

Avery nudged him with an elbow. "Remember you have to keep quiet about it."

"Are you doubting me?"

"No," Avery said, love for him filling her with hope. "Not in the least."

The alert came in as they were driving home. Even as Avery pulled the phone out of her purse, Judson drove faster. "I can't see anything," she said, calling up the app to look at the screen.

"Try a different angle."

"I am. Nothing. The screen's not clear."

"Could be snow on the lens."

"Mama," Brenna cried from the back seat when Judson hit a pothole. Avery reached behind her to run a soothing hand down Brenna's leg.

"Sorry," he said, not taking his eyes off the road ahead.

"Should I alert the sheriff?"

"Not yet. Let's see what we can find out first."

The house looked the same as it had when Judson had picked them up. Lights, on timers, were scattered throughout the interior. The outside security lights all blazed.

"Stay in the car," Judson said, getting out before Avery could argue.

She clutched her phone, ready to call for help if needed, as he disappeared around the back of the house. Her breath came out slow and long when he returned. "Nothing but horse tracks."

"So, it could have been anyone. Wait—" She gripped his arm when he put the car into gear. "What are you doing?"

His eyes were alive with fury, his nostrils flaring. "They weren't that far ahead of us."

"Judson, you can't be serious. We have no way of knowing which direction they went. We can't just ride around in the dark."

"I know where I'm heading."

"No." She jerked open her door.

"Avery." She heard his oath when she opened Brenna's door. "You can't be serious."

"They didn't get inside." She looked at him. "The alarm did its job of scaring them away."

"This time," he mumbled.

She slammed the door and marched to the house, not looking back when she heard Judson do the same. "I'm cold. I'm mad. And I want a damn glass of wine."

"Damn," Brenna repeated.

Avery choked back a laugh. "Baby . . ." She pressed her forehead to her daughter's. "That's a bad word. Mama was bad."

"Love Mama." Brenna kissed Avery's cheek, then reached out for Judson to take her. "Love, 'Udson," she said and kissed his cheek too. "Scratchy."

In the glow of the back porch light, it was a moment she would never forget. Her daughter's innocent declaration shot through his anger, and cleared the way for love. But it created a problem for Avery. Not the obvious one—the strong bond between Judson and Brenna. She would always be grateful her daughter had this first taste of what it felt like to have a loving masculine presence in her life.

But how could she consider selling the land and moving her daughter away? And yet, though she hated to admit it to herself, she was afraid that if she didn't sell Judson the land, she could lose him.

"Let's go inside," she said, softly.

THE NEXT MORNING, while downing his third cup of coffee, Judson walked the perimeter of Avery's house. After Gabriella's pregnancy announcement, the mad rush to the house and—he rubbed a hand over the skip in his chest—Brenna's sweet declaration, he'd slept little. Even with the warm comfort of Avery tucked against him.

Having her there is what kept his mind busy.

He wanted more than the occasional night together, even if

those nights were starting to become more frequent than ones spent apart. He didn't want to be a temporary part of her life. He wanted what Melanie had kept from him. He wanted a family, a future.

Did he want Avery's land to be part of that future? He couldn't deny the answer was yes. Was he willing to resort to threatening tactics to pressure her into selling? Never. That wasn't his style. But it was Daniel's.

From the beginning, he'd worried about how Daniel's interest in Avery's land would impact his own desire to purchase the property. Hearing that Daniel's daughter believed her father's interest had taken a turn toward the personal didn't mean Daniel had given up on the land. In fact, it had crossed Judson's mind that perhaps Daniel was hoping a personal involvement would convince Avery to sell to him.

When had his own attitude changed? When—he rubbed again at the kick in his chest—had he fallen in love with her?

The first night they'd made love? Before that? When she'd gotten sick, when Frances put something in her coffee? When her face had lit up as bright as the Christmas tree lights when he'd asked her to help him plan a party? Because wasn't hosting a Christmas party something a couple would do? He wanted that sense of belonging, of sharing and making memories. Starting and growing the traditions she so often mentioned. For Christmas, and throughout the year.

He couldn't imagine them not being together, day in and day out. He didn't want to imagine crawling into a bed he didn't share with her, eating a thrown-together sandwich while standing at the window rather than sitting at the table, sharing a meal. He wanted to know that when he came inside after a hard day's work, she'd be here to kiss him hello, tell him about her day, and share whatever chores were needed for Brenna. He wanted Christmases filled with decorations, trees, and more warmth than he'd known possible.

Hell, she'd even managed to bridge an ages-old gulf between him and his father.

Rising from where he'd crouched to study the horseshoe

prints, he decided to tell her he no longer wanted her land. At least, not only her land. He'd find another way to make the deal with Jacob Reece if need be. And if he couldn't, well he had plenty at the ranch to build on. Besides he'd have something more valuable than reputation or land—he'd have Avery and Brenna in his life.

As he entered the cabin, he heard the Christmas music, smelled the scent of coffee and bacon that lingered in the air from breakfast. From where he sat to remove his boots, he could see the reflected glow of the Christmas tree lights.

Yes, he thought. She could keep the land. And this cabin could double as her work studio. Or, he grinned at the idea, a little private getaway for the two of them from time to time.

He found her sitting on the floor, staring at the tree, her phone in her lap. Close by, Brenna stacked brightly colored blocks. "Play, Mama." Avery remained still and silent.

"Avery?"

"'Udson, play."

He sat down beside her and knocked down her stack of blocks. With delighted glee, she began re-stacking them. "Avery?"

She blinked, looked at him. "Oh, Judson." She let out a long, slow breath, blinking as if coming out of a dream. "I'm sorry, did you say something?"

"Are you okay?"

"Fine." She smiled, glanced down at her phone, then back at him. "I'm fabulous."

"Well," he said, curling his hands at her waist. "I can agree with that."

"I didn't get the design contract—the one I was asked to submit."

"Uhm, okay," he said, not sure where she was heading with this.

"No, really it is." She kissed him again before sitting back down and taking his hands. "My design just wasn't what they had in mind for the advertising campaign. But—" Her eyes sparkled as he'd never seen before. For some reason, Judson felt his stomach clench in a tight ball.

"They have another project that they think I'll be perfect for."

"That's great, Avery."

"They want me to come to New York after the first of the year."

"New York?"

"Yes, to meet with the marketing team so I can get a clear idea of what they're looking for."

"So . . ." He swallowed. "You'll be moving?"

"No." She frowned. "I don't know. I don't have to. I can do the job through zoom meetings, email and take the odd quick trip, if need be."

When she looked away, his hopeful thoughts about their life together crashed, just as he'd done to Brenna's blocks seconds earlier. She said she wasn't sure, there was no requirement for her to move, but he imagined her career trajectory would increase if she worked on a daily, close basis with a marketing team. How could he expect her to stay here when she'd just got an opportunity she'd worked so hard to earn? A chance that she'd once before put aside out of love and duty.

Her best friend lived in New York. Between that, the career boost and all the educational and cultural activities for Brenna, why wouldn't she want to move there?

And, a part of his brain whispered, if she moved, maybe she'd sell him the land.

"I'm happy for you, Avery."

"Nothing's certain yet. I still need to put together some design proposals."

"Looks like Santa delivered you an early Christmas present." He lifted her hand and pressed his lips to her knuckles. "We should celebrate."

Chapter Twelve

THE MORNING OF Judson's Christmas party dawned bright with blue skies and warmer temperatures. Avery hoped the weather would brighten her mood before the guests arrived. She didn't understand why she felt down. Not only was there the exciting magic of Christmas and the anticipation of the party, but her life was good—better than it had been in years.

Brenna was thriving in the preschool class. Avery had been given an opportunity that could open doors for her future. There'd been no more disturbing incidents at the house. She had made friends here in Burton Springs . . .

And she had a man in her life who she loved.

The day she'd told Judson about the new design prospect, he'd seemed genuinely happy for her. They'd spent the day together, playing with Brenna in the snow, snuggling on the sofa watching a movie while she napped. They hadn't seen the end of the movie. And, to her surprise later in the afternoon, a dinner delivery arrived, complete with candlelight and champagne.

He'd asked questions about the upcoming designs, mentioned places in New York he'd visited years earlier along with a few of the cultural options the city provided. It had almost felt as if he was encouraging her to make the prospective move rather than celebrating the opportunity she'd been given.

In their latest phone call, Londyn had told her she was overreacting. But Avery had been distracted, especially when Londyn finally admitted she'd received another series of emails from her unhappy fan.

"Maybe she's right," Avery said to Brenna as she packed the small suitcase. She sat down and scooped her little girl onto her lap for a hug. "Just like I'm probably silly for feeling guilty about taking you to Brittany's so she can babysit you while mama has an adult overnight."

To offset her guilt, she devoted the morning to playing with Brenna before dropping her off at the Davis house where Brittany would babysit.

Arriving at Judson's house, she discovered Kathy's crew already moving and rearranging furniture and setting up a temporary bar in a corner of the room. Avery carried her bag upstairs, biting on her bottom lip when she passed the empty bedroom where Brenna had slept before. Then, she walked into Judson's bedroom to find the tree he'd bought glowing brightly by the sitting area.

He could pretend otherwise but she knew he had a soft spot for Christmas. Granted, that spot had been buried the past few years, and it added to her enjoyment to know she'd helped him regain some of the magic of the season.

Here, where everything seemed so clear, felt so right, where there were no doubts or issues between them, she could touch one of the red heart ornaments and whisper, "I love you, Judson."

JUDSON STOOD AT the bedroom door, watching Avery stare at the tree, saw her lift a fingertip to an ornament. Heard a whisper but not the words.

Was she making a wish? Running through a list of details for tonight? Questioning whether or not to leave Burton Springs? And him?

He'd considered what he would do if she left. He could offer to buy her land and go on with his plans for his breeding operation. He'd hope that someday the hollow in his heart could be filled by someone else. He'd even considered following her to New York–provided that was what she wanted. He'd made a living before in the city, a good one. While some of his skills were rusty, he could polish them and find a job, a purpose. And he'd have that life with her. Only, in his heart of hearts, whenever he thought of them—of him and her and Brenna as a family—it was here on this ranch where they'd already started building a lifetime of memories.

She'd brought this once empty house back to life. She'd listened when he talked of his plans for the ranch. She'd even added little touches to the house–those silly placemats in the shape of Santa's hat on the kitchen table, a quilted tree skirt to replace the white sheet he'd tossed on the floor . . . The stockings she'd had embroidered with his and his father's names.

He wished he could propose to her, right here, right now. But that would be unfair to both of them. Instead, he vowed to give her, and him, a night to remember–no matter what the future brought.

"I can't decide." He smiled when she turned. "If you're regretting agreeing to this party. Or trying not to cry about leaving Brenna with a sitter."

"Maybe I'm thinking about all the dancing I hope to do tonight." Tilting her head, she gave him a flirty look, her eyes sparkling with amusement. "I've been told Carl at the Brewed Bean is an exceptional dancer."

"His partner is even better."

"Then I'll make sure to ask them both to dance."

"We should practice so we don't look bad as hosts."

"You seem smooth to me," Avery told him as he took her in his arms and they moved to the imaginary music.

"My mother taught me."

"Really? That's so sweet." She looked up at him. "Who was the first girl you danced with?"

"Kathy Davis."

"Really?"

"It was the school dance at the end of eighth grade. She wanted to get Dwight's attention so she asked me to dance with her. Before the next song started, they were together." With a grin he dipped her, earning a laugh. "But, every year at the Founders Day dance, I make sure I ask her."

"Oh, you'll have to make sure you ask her tonight, then."

"Only if you save the first dance for me."

"I'd have been insulted if you didn't ask." She settled her head in the crook of his shoulder. "I want this to be a night to remember."

He fought the feeling that her words were a kind of goodbye. Holding her close, but not as tight as he wanted, he spun them around the room until she laughed.

"Okay," she said, stepping away, her breath coming in fast pants. "You need to leave." She held up a hand when he stepped forward. "I mean it, Judson. I have things I need to do to get ready for tonight."

"So do I." He tugged his shirt free and moved his hands to his belt. He wanted to have every moment possible with her, make as many memories as they could. "Consider this like deciding where to hang the mistletoe. Or a practice dance." She snorted but he caught that sexy gleam come into her eyes when he flicked open the button on his jeans.

When he stepped forward, he took her face in his hands and tenderly kissed her. Time slowed. There was no hurried rush to strip, no fevered push to completion. Neither the past or the future intruded on their time. They had the luxury of knowing what each other liked, the beauty of giving without restraint. Slow hands caressed, gentle mouths enticed, hearts raced as one.

They had loved like this before, but never had it meant as much to him as it did today. As if they had all day, or the rest of their lives, they just held and kissed, content to simply be together. Judson didn't want to end, so he got a hard grip on his control and urged her toward peak. They moved as if through water, slowly, fluidly, bodies brushing, meeting. Until it became impossible to hold back their shared release.

When she started to move away from him, his hands kept her in place. "Just a little longer," he said.

"You've already put me behind schedule." But she stayed where she was.

"Have you already made plans for the trip to New York?"

"Nothing definite. Londyn's excited. She's looking forward to spending time with Brenna."

"What would you say if . . ."

"Avery?" someone called up the stairs.

She jerked upright. "Oh, no," she whispered, then cleared

her throat. "Be right down, Kathy. I'm just putting a few things away."

"No problem. I'll be in the kitchen."

"She knows," Avery hissed. "She knows exactly what we've been doing up here."

Before she could leave the bed, he had her back on her back, and was grinning down at her.

"Judson," she whispered. "We can't. Kathy's downstairs."

"Avery." He eased into her. "Look at that. Not only can we, we are." She moaned, but it sounded more encouraging than dismissive. Especially since she arched her hips just enough to allow him to sink deeper. "As long as she stays downstairs, everything will be fine."

She made him go out through the sliding doors leading off the upper balcony and down the outside stairs to the deck. As he passed by the kitchen window, he caught a glimpse of Kathy, who waved. With a flick of the brim of his hat, he went out to the barn.

"I don't get it," Judson complained two hours later, still in the barn where he and Hodge had been sent so they could have a cold cut sandwich and coffee from a thermos for lunch. "I know the people coming tonight. She knows them, too. It's not like I haven't been to a party with them before. What's so special about tonight?"

"If you can figure out a woman's mind, you're a better man than me. But—" Hodge broke off a bite of his sandwich and tossed it to Ginger. "There is something about Christmas that gets a woman all crazed up."

"I don't remember Mom ever acting like this."

Hodge chuckled, a clear sound of amusement, without any coughing or hacking to spoil it. "Boy, don't you remember how she'd sit up until late at night, crocheting all those scarfs and blankets she donated? And how she'd spend hours on those cookies you like, making sure they were as near to a real candy cane size and shape as she could get them."

"You ate them too."

"Sure did. The ones Avery made tasted just as good." Hodge

chuckled again. "Even the ones that weren't exactly a candy cane shape." Finished with his lunch, he reached into his shirt pocket in a habit Judson had seen all his life, then sighed when he came up empty now that he no longer carried a pack of cigarettes, or two, around with him.

"Seems to me there are worse things than a woman who wants your house to look nice for friends, who wants to make sure there's plenty of food and drink to go around." He paused, cleared his throat. "There's something to be said for having a woman—a special one—beside you every night."

"She might be moving," Judson said, keeping his voice as neutral as he could. "She's got this opportunity with a company in New York. She's going there after the first of the year to meet with the executives and talk about the project."

"A meeting's a long way from moving."

"A meeting's the first step in moving."

"With her being gone, that would clear the way for you to buy her land."

Judson swung around to glare at his father. "She means more to me than the land."

Hodge nodded. "Thought so."

"What's that supposed to mean?"

"If I have to tell you, then you're not as smart as I figured."

Shaking his head, Hodge went into the back room to work on a special Christmas present he was making. Judson cleaned stalls and gave the horses some extra attention. Usually, the chores were routine enough that he could let his mind wander, think things over, but today he kept his mind on the work.

A couple of hours later, Kathy walked into the barn, where Judson was now tossing a ball for Ginger. "I'm going home to change." Kathy walked over. She pointed a finger at him. "You keep that dog out of the house. Your guests don't want to go home covered in dog hair."

"Most of them have a dog."

"You mind what I said." She smiled. "Your house looks wonderful, Judson. Festive and bright."

"Seems like a lot of trouble for one night."

"A special night." She squeezed his arm. "It's nice to see you and Avery together." She released him and starting walking to her car. "Now, you'd better go inside and get cleaned up. I'll see you in a bit."

He took Ginger to his father's place, explaining Kathy's demand. It was hard to resent his father's chuckle when excitement began to stir in his stomach. Or maybe, as he went into the kitchen, it was the glorious odors that filled the room, and finding Ellen, the cook at Evergreen Ranch, behind the counter.

"Hey. I didn't realize you were in charge of the food tonight. I thought you'd be here with dancing shoes on, not an apron."

"I'm just delivering these few dishes. I'm about to head back to Evergreen and change."

He sent her a hopeful smile. "Need a taste-tester before you leave?"

"Avery warned me you would try to sneak a bite." She filled a plate with what he recognized as antojitos, one of his personal favorites, and three meatballs swimming in a red sauce. "Here, this should hold you."

"Good," he told her, taking a bite of the sliced tortilla shell filled with spicy cheese. "But I expected nothing less."

"Don't be using flattery to get more."

"It's not flattery, it's the truth."

"Go on." She took the empty plate from him, then studied him, head to toe. "You need a shower."

"Can't argue there. Save me a dance later?"

Her cheeks pink, Ellen nodded.

He stopped in the center of the great room. He'd almost become used to the lights and Christmas decorations, but tonight, the room sparkled. No, he corrected, it was filled with warmth. Not just from the fire burning in the fireplace, but from all that she'd done to make tonight special.

There was garland and bows, a dozen candles in different sizes and holders, ready to be lit. Tables with snowy cloths, centered by long ribbons of red and green, lined the walls, waiting to hold dishes of mouthwatering food. In one corner, a man he didn't recognize wearing a red bow tie in contrast to his white shirt, stood behind a portable bar, arranging bottles and glasses.

"Good evening, sir," he said when Judson approached. "Would you like a drink before your guests arrive?"

Before Judson could answer, he watched the young man's gaze move over his shoulder. Following the look, and hearing the bartender's low whistle of appreciation, Judson felt his throat close and his stomach fall.

She came down the stairs in high heels that did incredible things to legs he already considered amazing. The dress, as green as the Christmas tree, emphasized her slim build. It would flare, he decided, above her knees as she danced. She'd put her hair up, exposing the neck he liked to nibble on. Red stones dangled from her ears on thin strands of silver and he suddenly remembered her telling him about the lingerie she'd bought. And if all that wasn't enough, she smiled shyly as she did a slow turn.

Judson's world tipped on its axis. The dress dipped down, exposing her back almost to her waist. Whatever lingerie she wore, there couldn't be much of it.

She looked the way he imagined she'd often dressed for parties in her old life in Atlanta. The way she would if she moved to New York. Elegance wasn't something that came through just in clothing or jewelry. It was an innate part of her.

"The lady," he told the bartender without taking his eyes off Avery, "will have champagne."

AVERY WATCHED as Judson walked her way.

In jeans and flannel shirt, his hair matted from his hat, he moved with a sensuous grace. The champagne flute looked fragile, yet safe in his hands. As she so often felt.

Her heart pounded, sending her blood racing. While dressing, she thought of this moment, wondering what his reaction would be. What she saw in his dark eyes—appreciation, respect, and more than a little lust—surpassed anything she could have imagined.

"The house looks wonderful." He handed her the flute, wrapping his fingers around hers. She could feel his pulse and was thrilled to know it matched the pace of her own. "But you... You look amazing." He leaned in and gave her a kiss that was light, yet filled with promise.

When he drew back, his gaze stroked over her, as if stripping her to uncover what she wore underneath. "Red?" he asked.

Enjoying herself, she sipped champagne, eyeing him over the rim. "Red," she confirmed.

"I love Christmas."

She laughed. "Oh, God, Judson. I really want to hug you, but you smell of the barn." She sipped more champagne. "Go and get cleaned up so I can."

He leaned forward again, whispering in her ear, "Only if you promise we'll get dirty later tonight."

When he walked away, she struggled to not turn a circle in giddy delight. She'd so wanted to surprise him, and yes, tempt him. And later tonight, she fully intended to seduce him. But, until then, there were a few details to look over before their guests arrived, filling the house with Christmas magic.

Taking her glass with her, Avery headed into the kitchen. It took hardly more than a glance to realize she wasn't needed. The caterer and waitstaff that Kathy hired had everything under control.

"Excuse me," Avery asked the head cook, a blond woman with several tattoos, including one with a rose and knife crossed, adorning both arms. "I hate to ruin your presentation, but would it be possible to put together a to-go plate for me? Mr. Ford's father has decided against joining us tonight." Despite her numerous requests. "I'd like to at least make sure he tastes the food."

"No problem. We can fill a plate from the overflow dishes we have on the warming trays. What would he like?"

Avery smiled. "I trust you to choose. I'll just get my coat so I can take it out to him. He lives in a room behind the barn so I'll be back in no time."

"Oh, no. You can't go outside dressed like that. Great dress, but you don't want to be walking in the snow with those heels. None of the guests have arrived yet so Bobby can take a break from behind the bar and run a plate out to him."

With nothing else to do, Avery returned to the great room. Pacing, she made a quick call to Brittany, pleased when the babysitter confirmed Brenna had gone to sleep with no trouble. Not wanting to stare at the clock, she crossed the room and started the music, a low instrumental that would set the mood without restricting conversation.

Humming, she closed her eyes when she felt Judson's arms wrap around her waist, drawing her back to his chest.

"This isn't the first dance," he growled in her ear, making her shiver.

"Then what is it?"

"Just you and me."

"I like just you and me."

"Then why are we standing here waiting for a bunch of people to arrive?"

She laughed. "You can't fool me. You're looking forward to the party as much as I am." She turned in his arms, and her heart swelled. "Oh, Judson. You look wonderful."

His suit was as dark as his hair. The white shirt set off his natural tan and rugged good looks. She smiled when she saw his red tie—it was covered with Santa Claus figures.

"Don't get used to it."

She kissed his cheeks, then lingered at his mouth. "I can think of nothing I want more than to strip you out of this suit." She laughed and darted away when the doorbell rang. "But later, when we're alone." She reached for his hand and pulled him with her toward the front door.

"Promise," he asked.

"Absolutely." With a wide smile, she opened the door to Carter and Audra Montgomery. "Merry Christmas. Welcome."

The house was soon filled with friends—the laughter easy, the food and drinks enjoyed. Judson rarely left her side, or let go of her hand. And when they danced that first dance, a happiness she hadn't known possible spun with them.

Hours later, when the last good-bye had been said, and the caterer and crew had finished the kitchen clean-up, Avery walked over to Judson. Sliding her arms around his neck, she kissed him. "Will you dance once more with me?"

His hand was warm where her dress exposed her bare back. His eyes were dark and focused as he stared at her. His lips, when they brushed over hers, were soft and thrilling.

"It was such a wonderful night."

"I like the ornaments you gave everyone. Especially since you used string as the hanger," he said, dancing them closer to the tree where a new rocking horse ornament hung.

"Your father cut them out."

"Did he?"

She nodded. "You're right, he's good with wood. It was his design and he sanded them, but I stained them and added the year."

"What do you have in mind for next year?"

It warmed her that he was already thinking they would host another party. "Maybe a bell." She released two buttons on his shirt, arching a little when his hand dipped under the back opening of her dress. A lone fingertip traced the band of her thong. "Maybe we should head upstairs and, uhm, discuss it."

"I'm sorry." A voice broke the silence.

"What is going on today? Can't a man seduce a sexy woman in his own home without interruption?" Judson whispered before looking over his shoulder.

"We're through with the clean-up," the caterer said. "I thought you would want to lock up behind us."

"Go ahead," Avery told Judson, pulling the tie free of his collar and slipping it over her neck. "I'll wait upstairs."

"Like this," he whispered.

She nodded, then walked away. "Judson?" she said, stopping at the foot of the stairs. "Why don't you bring along a bottle of champagne with you?"

THE MORNING AFTER the party, Avery woke up in Judson's

arms. And while she enjoyed it, it surprised her. He was usually up early, just out of long-time habit and the need to see to the animals. On the other hand, it was no wonder he slept. They'd loved until nearly dawn. Few words had passed between them but love had been in every caress and kiss. At least in hers.

She'd been daring and demanding, more so than she'd believed herself capable of being. Together, they'd been open, so giving of trust. Still, as incredible as last night had been, it would have been so much more memorable if she'd felt free to say the words that drummed strong and true in her heart. And, better yet, to hear them given back to her.

Why not tell him she loved him? There was nothing to lose by voicing the words. If he didn't return them, then wouldn't she be better off knowing the truth rather than holding out hope? She'd lived with one man who hadn't loved her. She couldn't do it again.

"Why did I let you talk me into this?" Avery asked later, after showers and a shared breakfast.

"Hey, don't pin this on me. It was your idea."

She frowned at the clipped argument. It was the way he'd been most of the morning. While she could blame his foul mood on fatigue, she couldn't accept being the target.. "But you said—"

"I said I would go with you to pick up Brenna. You're the one who suggested the side trip."

"You said it couldn't do any harm." She watched her daughter laugh as, beneath the shelter of an open-ended shed, six of the puppies Ed had told Avery about crawled over her, all fighting for her attention. "I'm going to give in. You and I both know it."

"You can't."

Surprised again by his curtness, Avery looked back at Judson. "What do you mean?"

"These pups, they aren't going to stay little like this."

"I know that."

"A dog like that would be fine for her if you stayed here, where there's room for it to run. But what about New York?

Most apartments don't have yard space, let alone enough indoor room for a dog this size needs."

"And if I don't move?"

"Why wouldn't you? That's the kind of life you wanted all those years ago before you stayed to care for your father. You've got nothing stopping you now."

Except love.

He made it sound as if she'd already decided, as if he had no trouble letting her leave. She turned away, using the pretense of watching Brenna play to avoid looking at him. After the night they'd shared, the sense of community and friendship as much as the intimacy, she'd thought they'd built a foundation for the future. Now he was all but suggesting she pack her bags.

Why the sudden change in his attitude? Was it because her decision about selling the land and this new potential career move had the same deadline? One that was rapidly approaching. Had everything between them simply been temporary, on his end, leading up to this point? She felt something like a streak of grief slice through her. Would no one ever want her for herself?

The vibration in her coat pocket had her drawing out her phone and a new concern raised its ugly head. *Unknown caller.* She hit dismiss. Before she could shove the phone back in her pocket, it vibrated again. *Unknown caller.*

"Something wrong?" Judson asked.

"No." She turned back, pressing the phone to her chest.

"If it's about your work, go ahead. I'm sure it must be important."

He walked over to squat down beside Brenna. She stared, blinking back tears at the abruptly cool, and up to this instant, totally uncharacteristic, dismissal. It also gave her another uncomfortable thought. Whatever his feelings for her, she knew he adored her daughter. Was he using Brenna as a substitute for the child he'd been denied?

The phone again vibrated. "Hello?"

"You haven't left," came the muffled voice. Avery's dry throat prevented her from responding. "It's going to get worse if you don't."

"What are you saying?" she whispered.

"Your little girl sure is cute in that pink coat."

When the phone went dead, Avery swung around, nearly crying out in panic when she didn't spot Brenna. Then she saw her beside Judson where they had crossed the yard to look at the goats on the other side of a wire fence.

"Ready to go home?"

"No, Mama. I want play puppies."

"The puppies need a nap. And so do you."

"Not tired."

"We're going home, Brenna. Now."

Judson lifted a brow, looking at a pouting Brenna, but said nothing. The ride to her house was silent, so different from their past times together. Avery understood part of her reserve was worry over the phone calls, her indecision about telling Judson. Only, his silence kept her from confiding in him. At the house, it didn't surprise her that he didn't unbuckle Brenna from her car seat the way he'd gotten into the habit of doing. It was something that Avery admitted she'd become spoiled by.

"'Udson," Brenna said.

It broke her heart to hear Brenna's confusion in her voice when Judson drove away after little more than a brief good-bye.

"He has to go home," Avery said.

The house felt cold and lonely. When Brenna resisted going down for a nap—and Avery wanted the comfort of her daughter anyway—she climbed into bed with her, reading until Brenna fell asleep. Before long, her late night caught up with her and she fell into a nap that ran rampant with dark images.

For the next two days she kept busy with work, easing Brenna's distress over missing Judson, Hodge, and Ginger, and checking in with Londyn. She ignored every *Unknown* phone call she received.

She was in the kitchen brewing tea while Brenna napped when she heard a truck approach. Foolish hope that Judson had come to see her died when she recognized Daniel's vehicle. She shut off the security system and opened the door before he could knock.

"Hello, Avery." He took off his hat, smoothing a hand over his hair. He looked nervous, which did nothing to help her nerves.

"Hello, Daniel. Come in out of the cold."

It crossed her mind that Judson had never used her front door. Nor had she used his. They'd both entered through the back door; the way good friends, family, or a lover, would always know was open to them.

He scanned the room. "Are you alone?"

"I was making some tea." She extended a hand, indicating he should walk before her. "Would you care for any?"

"Thank you."

She waited until he'd removed his coat and sat before she turned to the stove where the kettle was boiling. "What brings you out here today, Daniel?"

"I wanted to see you."

She glanced over her shoulder. His gaze held hers, a less intense look than he'd given her in the past. Still, she didn't completely relax. She didn't want to misread his intentions the way it appeared she'd done with Judson. Pouring water from the kettle into the mugs, she plated a few cookies.

"Are you ready for Christmas?" she asked, joining him at the table.

"I'm afraid there isn't much to do. Frances gives me a list of things she'd like." He chuckled. "Including where to buy everything. I just place the orders."

"No surprises from Santa, then?"

"It's hard to surprise a sixteen-year-old daughter."

God, she hoped not. She hoped every year, no matter her age, Brenna found a special package from Santa under the tree. Annoyed by the longing, she shut down the image of sitting beside the tree with Judson.

"I'm looking forward to watching Brenna open gifts on Christmas morning," she said. "This will be the first Christmas where she'll have any idea of what's going on." She absently nibbled on a cookie. "I imagine us staying in our pajamas all day, playing with her toys, eating cookies for breakfast." She shook her head. "Sorry, I tend to create scenes in my mind."

"Must be a byproduct of your graphic design business."

That he knew of her business didn't alarm her, but she also couldn't shake off a sudden prick of unease.

"I've heard you have an opportunity in New York." He shrugged when she stared at him, saying nothing. "Word I got was you're thinking of moving there." He cleared his throat and took a sip of his tea. "That's why I'm here. If you are moving, selling the land before the end of the year would give you additional funds to buy a nice place. And you'd avoid having to pay first quarter property taxes."

"Property taxes," she repeated.

"Look, I'm not going to lie—there's no point in it. You know I want your land. We both know Judson wants it, too. I'm willing to top whatever offer he makes."

"He hasn't made one."

"No?" Daniel frowned, but she caught the gleam of satisfaction that came into his eyes. "I was told he was signing loan papers at the bank the day before that party you hosted at his house. That's why I took the chance of coming out here."

"I see," she said, feeling sick to her stomach. The timing was too coincidental to be ignored. Judson had been moody and withdrawn since the morning after the party. "You've given me something to consider. My best friend lives in New York. Maybe I should take a quick trip to see her. While I'm there, I can check out what I might be able to afford."

He covered her hand, preventing her from rising. "I've always believed you to be a smart woman, Avery. If we make this deal, I want you to know you'll always be welcomed to visit The Golden G."

She wanted him out of her house, so she simply smiled and said, "Thank you."

As Daniel drove away, Avery slammed the front door hard enough that she woke Brenna. Which suited Avery's frame of mind just fine.

"Hey, baby. Want to go see Judson?" she asked, not above using whatever means necessary to confront Judson.

"'Udson. Doggie."

Her sense of betrayal and anger grew, along with a side dish of guilt for Brenna's excitement at seeing Judson, as she turned onto the road leading to his ranch. Why hadn't he told her he'd gone ahead and secured a loan? Was it even possible it had nothing to do with her land? Why had she had to learn about it from Daniel?

She braked to a stop, barely a foot away from Judson, and got out, slamming her car door on Brenna's exciting greeting.

"Something wrong?" he asked, his gaze taking in Brenna still in the back seat. "Did something happen?"

"Why didn't you tell me?"

"What the hell are you talking about? You're the one who came rushing out here like a rodeo horse chasing down a calf."

"No." She pointed a finger at him. "You don't get to be mad at me."

"Avery." He shook his head, drew in a long breath, as if trying to calm down. "I don't know what you want me to say."

"I want you to explain to me why you signed a bank loan."

Chapter Thirteen

HE DIDN'T HAVE to answer—she saw the guilt spread over his face.

"So, it's true."

"Ginger," he called to the dog currently softly barking at Brenna's door.

"Don't," Avery called out when Judson took a step toward her. She needed to leave. Before the tears scalding her eyes fell for him to see. It didn't matter what excuse he gave her. The bottom line was he hadn't trusted her enough to be honest.

"It makes sense now. The way you've talked about the wonderful opportunities New York would give both me and Brenna. The way you've all but packed my bags and drove me to the airport." She ignored his low oath. "Because we'd become lovers, you figured I'd sell to you if I moved."

"Avery, you've got it all wrong."

"You think I'd believe anything you said now?"

"Yet you believe the worse about me, because Gaines said something to you."

"He's never lied to me."

"What about all the accidents you've had at your house?"

"You mean the ones that you consistently said there was no point in telling the sheriff about because there was no proof? How did you know there was no proof? Because you'd made sure of it?"

"Now, wait a minute."

She spotted Hodge coming out of the barn and heard Brenna calling for all of them. Avery backed up, nearly tripping over Ginger, before she opened her car door.

"Mama."

"Not now, Brenna."

"Doggie, Mama. 'Udson. 'Odge."

Avery bit down on her lip to avoid screaming. It wasn't Brenna's fault she was upset. Avery had told her they were coming here. And Brenna had fallen in love with Judson, Hodge, and Ginger. As had Avery.

That was why she needed to get away. Before she gave him a chance to explain and love prompted her to believe whatever he said. Tears flooding her eyes as she drove away, she concentrated on the road and refused to look in the rearview mirror.

Back at her house, she cuddled her daughter until Brenna settled down. Then, deciding she wanted some distance and time, she packed a couple of bags and a tote filled with toys, and loaded them in her SUV. "Let's go on a trip," she told Brenna as she belted her in her car seat.

"See 'Udson?"

Rather than listen to cries of disappointment, Avery didn't answer. "Look, Brenna," she said as she drove into town. "Lights."

The sniffle that came from the back seat tore her heart into two. "Here we are." She parked and opened Brenna's door.

"Want 'Udson, mama."

Undone, Avery pressed her forehead to Brenna's. "Oh, baby, me too."

"Need some help?"

Jerking up, Avery banged her head on the door frame.

"Sorry about that," Kendall Montgomery said when Avery looked over at her, rubbing the top of her head. Kendall's cop gaze skimmed over the bags in the cargo area. "Going somewhere?"

"Just wanted a change of scenery for a few days. Gabriella told me I could use the apartment if I wanted."

"What is it about this place that makes that apartment the perfect place to run away to?"

Kendall detailed a story from the month before when a six-year-old ran away from home and hid in the apartment, where her first-grade teacher was living while doing her student teaching. She held Brenna while Avery entered the code on the keypad and they went inside.

"How long are you planning to stay?" She held up a hand. "I'm not asking for an explanation or gossip. I just want to alert the rest of the department."

That kind of decision felt beyond Avery's capability right now. All she wanted was time and silence to escape the hurt.

"Why don't I let you know when I leave?"

FROM A HILLTOP, through a pair of binoculars, a pair of curious eyes had watched Avery McClain drive away. So, Daniel's assertion that the woman intended to leave for a few days appeared correct. He seemed confident that when she returned, she'd sell the land.

Especially if the land was all she had left.

"WHAT WAS THAT all about?" Hodge asked as he approached Judson, who stared after Avery's SUV.

"Gaines," he spat out.

"What'd he do now?"

"He told Avery I'd been to the bank to inquire about a loan."

"Had you?"

"I'm not talking about this in the freezing cold." He headed for the house, making no comment when Hodge followed. In the kitchen, Judson went to the cupboard and pulled down a bottle of whiskey.

"Think that's going to help?" Hodge asked.

"Can't hurt."

He poured two fingers, downed it in one swallow, relishing the burn as it slid down his throat. Maybe it would chase away the memory of the tears Avery had tried so hard not to let him see. Pouring more whiskey, he studied the liquid.

"I went to the bank to see about a loan in case Avery took the job in New York."

"To buy her land."

"No. I wanted the money to live on until I could find a job there. That is, if she let me go with her. That's why I got so impatient with her the day we went to look at the pups. I thought there was a chance she'd stay here. But I realized I had to let her go. She deserves this career opportunity, and I won't do anything to keep her from having what she wants." He turned away from the liquor, faced his father. "I'd already talked with Harley and signed papers to give you control of the day-to-day running of the ranch."

"Now, why did you do a damned fool thing like that?"

"You're my father. Who else would I trust to take care of things around here if I leave?"

Hodge ran a hand over his mouth. "You gave me a place to stay and work, even when you resented me for your mother's death. There have been times when I wondered if it was to punish me, to remind me every day of everything I did wrong." He glanced around the room, and Judson realized it was the first time his father had been inside his house. "There were times I figured it was no less than I deserved."

Honestly stunned, and hurt, Judson swallowed hard.

"Before I go on, I want you to know I'm proud of what you have here. You've worked hard to build a good reputation. But, son, you think I like knowing you've been every bit as alone as I am? That you don't wish you had someone to share your life with? I thought you'd found that with Avery."

So had I, Judson thought, but remained quiet.

"You always did only see your side of things."

"What's that supposed to mean?"

Hodge patted his shirt pocket before he dropped his hand to his side. Judson wondered how long his father would continue to reach for the absent cigarettes.

"It means you've always planned for the way you think things should go. It's one reason why you've done a better job with this ranch then I ever did with ours. This time, I figure, you planned to wait for Avery to tell you she was moving, and then you'd tell her you wanted to go with her."

"I was going to ask if she wanted me to come along," Judson said, even though Hodge had pretty much nailed it on the head.

"Maybe, but I gotta say, I can't see you going back to a city and being happy after all you've built here. And I mean more than the ranch and the breeding. You've got friends here, good ones, that care about you, that mean something to you. But you went ahead with those plans, and didn't bother to tell her."

"She didn't give me a chance. She came out here, mad and accusing me of things that aren't true."

"What else was she supposed to do when you hadn't told her what you want? Or why you'd done what she'd learned about? When you hadn't told her that you love her."

Judson jammed his hands in his back pockets. It had been a long time since he'd been on the receiving end of this kind of talk from his father. And longer still since he'd taken the time to listen.

"You didn't give her a chance to tell you what she wants. What if she doesn't want to leave here?"

"But her job—"

"She can do her job anywhere is what she told me. She said it was one of the perks of working for herself instead of a company, and she liked the freedom to work at home so she could be with Brenna. Didn't she put together that fancy website for you?"

"This is different."

"Why?" Hodge nodded when Judson opened his mouth, only to shut it. "Your way," he said. "Just like this bull about me taking over the running of this ranch. Maybe I don't want to be in charge."

Judson watched, shocked to see tears come into his father's eyes. "It took us a helluva long time to get so we can talk without angry words between us. Maybe I don't want to work this ranch without you around."

Hodge then did something he hadn't done since Judson was ten. He pulled him close for a hard hug. "Talk to Avery. Ask her about her side of things." He stepped back. "Then, I'll stand by you, whatever you decide to do." Then he walked away.

Alone, Judson returned the whiskey bottle to the cabinet and started to put the glass in the dishwasher. When he realized it was full of clean dishes, he left the glass on the countertop.

With Ginger at his heels, he walked into the great room. And came to a stop.

The bright lights on the Christmas tree mocked him. He shut his eyes but it was worse as his mind filled with images of Avery laughing because he'd forgotten to get the hangers for the ornaments. Avery standing beside the tree, letting her nightgown fall to the floor. Swearing, he raced up the stairs to take a shower.

No matter where he went or what he did, there were reminders of her. The Christmas tree he'd bought and placed in the sitting area. On the dresser was the small crystal dish where she'd left the silver hoops she'd worn the day before. Her shampoo was still in the shower, the peach scent he knew would always remind him of her.

How was it that with the house empty, he couldn't enter a room without something reminding him of her?

He took Ginger outside, thinking the fresh air would be good for both of them. Only Ginger had no interest in chasing the ball Judson threw. Instead, she sat beside him, giving him looks that clearly said she thought this was all his fault.

Judson stared at the lights he'd strung along the house and barn, recalling Brenna's delight. As if reading his mind, Ginger pressed against his leg, whining.

"I know you miss them too." He patted her head. "But there's nothing we can do tonight." When he started for the house, Ginger stopped in front of him. "Look, I told you . . ." The dog barked, loud and long enough that it brought Hodge outside.

"What's the matter with her?"

"Hell, if I know," Judson said. "Every time I start for the house, she blocks me."

"Think there's a coyote prowling around?"

"If so, I don't want it coming after Ginger."

The dog ran to his truck and waited by his door. Losing patience, Judson was about to drag her away when the phone in his back pocket buzzed. Looking at it, he saw the alarm alert.

"Something's happening at Avery's," he told Hodge, running to the truck.

"Give me a minute," Hodge called out. "I'll come along."

"Not waiting. I'll call as soon as I know something."

As he drove through the night, a sense of urgency grabbed him and increased his speed. The night was quiet but his heart was pounding. Whether it was from anticipation or fear, he couldn't be sure.

Cresting the hill that led to her house, he saw a flicker of light. Was that a candle burning? A fire in the fireplace while she sat and cursed him? Then he saw the light climb higher and realized it was a flame. Ginger began to bark.

Fire.

He floored the accelerator, sending the truck into a swerving race through the mush of the melted snow and skidding on ice. Finally, he slammed on breaks, skidding more, shoving the truck into park. "Stay," he commanded, jumping out, leaving the engine running.

He banged on the back door, but got no response. Looking around, he spotted a shovel. He grabbed it, using it to smash open the window so he could reach in and unlock the door.

"Avery? Ginger, no," he said when the dog tried to nose past him. He took precious time holding her back.

"911, what's your emergency?"

"Rhonda, it's Judson's. Avery's house is on fire. Get someone here. I'm going in to get her and Brenna out."

"Wait—"

"The hell I will." Shoving his phone in his pocket, he told Ginger to stay. She whined, but he turned back to the house and entered the back mudroom. Smoke was thick enough that he lowered to the floor and belly-crawled down the hall. In the great room he saw her tree and the colorful presents below the lowest branches, in flames.

"Avery," he called out again. "Brenna."

All he heard was the roar of fire. His heart hammered as he moved as quickly as possible, using the baseboard, and his memory, as guide. The crash of her Christmas tree had him jumping, then crawling faster. Reaching the opening of a doorway, he went into the bedroom that had been painted lavender rather than the typical little-girl-pink.

Swallowing a mouthful of smoke as he called her name meant he had to pause and try to clear this throat by coughing. Tears burned his eyes but he kept moving in the direction of her bed. He ignored the buzz of his phone in his back pocket as he crawled up the mattress, only to discover, after stretching over the entire length and width, that it was empty. While retracing his crawl out of the bedroom, a multitude of oaths, and prayers, ran through his mind.

"Avery."

Pausing in the doorway, he scanned the hall as best he could through the smoke. He could see the bright orange and red glow of the fire, felt the heat of it on his skin and searing his throat, lungs, and eyes. He pushed forward, heading for Avery's bedroom, hoping he'd find them and fighting to stay ahead of the fear he'd be too late.

He should have paid attention to Ginger in the beginning. He should have immediately chased after Avery when she left. Hell, he should never have let her leave in the first place.

"Avery," he yelled at the top of his lungs. He lost precious moments when he had to stop and cough, spitting out a thick stream of mucus. He crawled faster, again calling out Avery's name, when he reached her bedroom. Once again, a search of the bed came up empty.

"No," he shouted, burying his face in her pillow. This was the bed where they'd first made love. He remembered how she'd looked, arms open, trust in her gaze, accepting him. She'd been so generous, so loving that night. And every day and night they'd been together.

She was a fighter. Wasn't that why she was in Burton Springs in the first place? She hadn't allowed her husband's infidelity to destroy her, and had fought back when he'd tried to take her inheritance. She'd made sure her daughter knew love despite her father's cruel dismissal.

Hell, wasn't that why he was here searching for them? Because she'd been strong enough to confront him about his lack of honesty? Because he'd been so afraid of losing that he hadn't wanted to face the risk that she might choose a career over a life and family with him?

He'd lost the chance to tell her he loved her.

No. His head snapped up. He refused to give up. He *would* find them.

Again belly-crawling, he searched the bathroom, checking the shower and bathtub. Turning on water in the tub, he dunked his head, washing the smoke and ash from his face. He heard the thin wail of a siren and Ginger's barking.

Exhausted, grieving, he rested his cheek on the tile floor and closed his eyes.

He never felt the hands that carried him outside, didn't feel the hands that fitted him with oxygen. He only knew the feel of Ginger licking his face.

He sat up quickly, fighting the hands that tried to keep him still, tearing away the wires and tubes. "Let me go. I've got to find her," he said, stopping when his body exploded with wracking coughs.

"Judson." Kendall Montgomery squatted in front of him. "She's not here. She's at Gabriella's apartment. I promise she's safe. Her and Brenna. I'll get them and bring them to the hospital."

"My dad," he croaked out.

She nodded, then squeezed his hands. "You've got to relax now. Let the medics help you."

IT TOOK AVERY a minute to understand someone really was knocking at the door, that it wasn't a part of her fitful dream. Rolling off the sofa, she wrapped a blanket around her shoulders.

"Who is it?" she asked.

"Avery, it's Kendall. Let me in."

As she fumbled for the lock, Avery felt cold dread wash over her. "What's wrong?" she said as soon as the door opened. Her fear doubled when Kendall wrapped her in her arms.

"Judson's going to be fine."

"What happened?"

"There was a fire." Avery gasped, drew back to stare at

Kendall, who shook her head. "No, not his house. Yours, Avery."

When her legs crumbled, Kendall supported her until they could sit side-by-side on the sofa. "Judson suffered smoke inhalation while he was searching your house, trying to get you and Brenna out safe."

"Why? Why did he go there?" she asked, then recalled him saying he regretted not being able to help save his mother in a house fire. "Oh, Judson."

"I'm not sure. I didn't get to talk to him long. The medics wanted to get him to the hospital and, well, to be honest, he couldn't talk much without coughing." Avery rubbed trembling fingers up and down her own throat. "Let me get you a glass of water," Kendall offered.

She could have lost him. All because she hadn't given him a chance to explain. She loved him. Shouldn't she have asked, rather than accuse? Shouldn't she have trusted, rather than doubt?

"Avery," Kendall said after she'd swallowed two mouthfuls of the tepid liquid. "I don't know what happened between you and Judson that made you come here, but I've got to say, as a friend, not as a deputy, what I saw tonight was a man willing to do anything for the woman he loves." She smiled a little. "Remind me sometime to tell you why I know how that feels. Now, let's get you and Brenna dressed."

She moved on auto-pilot. While Avery dressed, Kendall woke and soothed a cranky Brenna. It wasn't until they were on their way to the hospital that Avery functioned. "Hodge," she said, whispering so Brenna didn't overhear.

"It's okay," Kendall reassured her. "I spoke with him. He'll be at the hospital. I also called Gabriella. She's going to contact the hospital and keep in touch with them about Judson's treatments."

So, there was nothing to do but sit and worry. When Kendall stopped in front of the hospital entrance, fear kept Avery still. Kendall unbuckled Brenna, then came around to open Avery's door.

"Why you cry, Mama?" Brenna asked, confused.

"I'm just tired, baby," Avery lied, wiping the tears from her eyes.

"Me tired too." Brenna yawned and held out her arms for her mother.

"I've got her," Avery said when Kendall went to take her. "I need something to hold onto."

Following Kendall, Avery walked into the waiting room.

"'Odge," Brenna cheerfully called out and she was so thankful that her little girl eased some of the stress she saw lined on the older man's face. "Doggie," she squealed when she spotted Ginger. Not knowing what else to do, Avery set Brenna down so she could run to the dog.

"They're letting her stay," Hodge said, referring to Ginger. "The sheriff is in with him. He said he wanted to see you as soon as you got here." He cleared his throat. "I'm not sure how much he'll be able to talk."

"Come sit down with me, Hodge." Taking his arm, she led them both to one of the hard plastic chairs. While they waited, the mayor and Kathy Davis appeared, bringing cups of coffee, and offering to get anything else anyone might need. When the sheriff joined them, Avery and Hodge stood.

"He gave me his phone," the sheriff said, handing the plastic bag holding Judson's phone to Kendall. "He's got video of the person who started the fire."

"Gaines?" Hodge asked.

"You know I can't say."

"Listen here, that's my boy in there. I'm not leaving here until he does, so you don't have to worry about me getting to Gaines before you."

"It's a Gaines," the sheriff admitted after a brief pause. "But not Daniel. It's his daughter, Frances." With a nod, he put on his hat. "He's asking to see you."

After an encouraging nod from Hodge, she pushed open the door of his room. The lights over the bed were bright, highlighting his pale face and still body. There was a tube connecting him to an IV and another at his nose to help him breathe. His chest rose and fell in a steady rhythm. When he turned toward her, she felt tears cloud her eyes at the sight of his red-rimmed ones.

"Oh, Judson."

He held out a hand and she ran to him, holding on tight. "You're okay," he croaked.

"Shh." She brushed hair off his forehead, pressed her lips there. "You need to rest your throat and voice."

"Need to tell you—"

"It can wait." She smiled at him. "I'm not going anywhere."

Throughout the long night, she stayed by his side whenever possible, occasionally switching places with Hodge. Kathy Davis took Brenna and Ginger to her house. Medical staff came and went, checking vitals, monitoring his oxygen levels, taking blood samples and a chest x-ray. Thankfully, he'd suffered no significant burns.

"Hold you," he said, stopping to cough.

She offered him the straw so he could drink some ice water. "Judson, you need to rest."

He patted the bed beside him. How could she deny him when it was what she wanted too? Careful to not tangle up his tubes, she stretched out beside him. "We'll probably get in trouble, you know."

"Worth it."

It was hard to argue when it felt good to be this close. She listened to the rasp of his breathing, thought again of how close she'd come to losing him. No property, no amount of pride, *nothing*, was worth that price. Maybe he hadn't told her about the loan. But when it counted, when he believed her and Brenna's life was on the line, he hadn't hesitated.

"I love you," she whispered as sleep claimed him.

A FEW HOURS LATER, the sheriff came in to check on Judson. He explained to Avery that thanks to Judson's security video, they knew just who was behind the fire.

"Wait a minute." Avery stopped the sheriff from leaving. "How did Judson have a video of my house on his phone?"

"He obviously has access to your security system."

Chapter Fourteen

JUDSON CURBED his impatience as the doctor rattled off more instructions. He wanted to go home.

He had a fuzzy memory of Avery whispering something as she lay beside him, softly enough that he hadn't been able to make out the words. Only when the nurse woke him this morning, he'd been alone. He hadn't seen her during the endless hours he spent waiting for release. Most of the day was gone, and he was just now going home.

"Do you understand, Mr. Ford?" Judson nodded at the doctor, not trying to speak and risk the doctor hearing how raw his throat still felt. Not to mention, he needed to save his voice for a couple of important conversations. He still couldn't get over how taking a shower had sapped his strength.

"I spoke with Doctor Ferguson." Judson blinked at him in surprise. "She'll do the follow-up on you when she returns from Chicago. In the meantime, try to talk as little as possible." At another nod, the doctor looked to Hodge. Judson knew his father had spent the night at the hospital. His dad looked tired but there was no odor indicating he'd lapsed into smoking away the stress.

"If you want to go down and drive your vehicle to the door, the nurse will be here shortly to wheel him down." The doctor held out a hand to both men with a small smile. "Merry Christmas."

"Dad." He reached out, stopping Hodge from leaving. "Where's Avery?"

"Damn it, Judson. Didn't you listen to a word that doctor said?" Judson just stared at him, seeing the fatigue and worry of a long night. Would it have been there—would either of them have this new closeness—without Avery in their life?

"Where?" he asked, sucking in a deep breath.

"She went to check on the little one."

Judson waited until they were in the truck before he held out his hand. "Phone."

"Damn stubborn fool."

"Just like my daddy."

Hodge chuckled as he offered the phone.

"Hodge?" Avery answered. "Is something wrong? Did Judson have a setback?"

"Avery."

"Oh, Judson."

He heard tears in her voice, found he had to battle his own. "Come home," he said. "Please."

"You need to rest."

"Need you."

"I'll be there."

"Give me that damn phone now," Hodge said when he ended the call.

"Minute." He had another, far more important call to make. When he finished, he dropped the phone onto the center console.

Annoyed by how the short conversation drained him, Judson sat back and closed his eyes. He didn't move when his father stopped the truck. "Be right back." When the door opened and closed a second time, he felt the cool wetness of a plastic bottle pressed into his hand. "Drink it all," Hodge said, putting a second bottle in the cup holder before he started driving again.

He took a drink, let the water sit at the back of his throat for a second before swallowing it down. By time they turned off the main road leading to the ranch, he'd polished off both bottles. The lights on the barn battled the darkening sky. He whispered an oath at the number of cars parked outside the back door.

How was he supposed to explain to Avery with all these people around?

Then the mudroom door opened and there she was. She looked terrific in a pair of jeans and a navy sweater. She rubbed her hands together in what he thought was due to nerves rather than the cold. He understood.

"Hey," he called out raggedly as he stepped out of the truck. "Looks like I'm missing the party."

"I couldn't talk them out of being here." He nodded, knowing he should have expected this show of friendship and support. No doubt his kitchen was filled with more food than they could eat in a month.

"Come inside before you get cold." She wrapped an arm around his waist. "I know how thin those scrubs are."

He just couldn't help it. He drew her close, wrapping both arms around her. "Feels good to be home," he whispered in her ear.

He leaned on her as they walked toward the house, not because he had to but because he wanted to. It lifted his spirits that she allowed it, just as it had when she'd crawled into the hospital bed with him.

"'Udson." Brenna, closely followed by Ginger, ran to him once he was inside. Rather than risk lifting her, Judson sat on the floor, laughing when Brenna climbed onto his lap and Ginger licked his face.

"'Udson hurt." His heart melted when she leaned forward and kissed his cheek. "Better?"

"Better," he confirmed, hugging her close.

"C'mon, Brenna." Avery pulled her away, then reached for his hands. "Judson needs to rest."

Neighbors and friends greeted him, offered words of praise for his actions and gratitude for his safety as he walked hand-in-hand with Avery. Then everyone grew quiet when Sheriff Owens walked inside.

"Judson. Good to see you up and about." He glanced around the room. "Is there somewhere we can talk in private?"

"Sheriff." Judson sat in his recliner, pleased when Avery stayed by his side. "These are friends and neighbors, many of them with ranches close by. I think they deserve to know what happened last night."

The sheriff looked as if he still planned to suggest a more private setting until Avery curled her hand on Judson's shoulder, presenting a united front.

"Based on your information, I went to The Golden G. Initially, Frances Gaines denied the accusation that she'd set fire to Ms. McClain's cabin. It was only when informed about you being taken to the hospital that she relented and confessed." He paused when the group whispered, and made a few louder, comments.

"She admitted she watched Avery load her car with luggage and drive away. She'd thought that if the house was gone, Avery would be more inclined to sell the land to her father. She believed he'd be proud of her."

"The phone calls." Avery frowned when the sheriff, and Judson, looked at her. "I received phone calls, maybe three, four? They all showed up on the caller ID as *Unknown*. The voice was disguised but each time they called, the person on the line told me to leave. The last time—" She looked at Judson. "It was the day we took Brenna to see the puppies. The caller said she looked cute in her pink coat."

"She must have been close by, watching."

"Can I take your phone in and see if our techs can find out where the calls originated?" the sheriff asked. When she retrieved her phone and handed it to him, he added, "I'll tell you, Daniel seemed rattled by his daughter's actions."

"Where is she?" Avery asked.

"Deputy Montgomery drove her to a juvenile facility where she'll go before a judge. He and the prosecuting attorney will then decide if the case should go to trial. More than likely, taking her confession and cooperation into consideration, the judge will take it easy on her. That is, unless you want to take things further."

"I don't think so, but thank you, Sheriff."

"It was your phone that sealed the deal, Judson." He felt Avery's fingers dig into his shoulder. "I'll keep you posted on any developments." The sheriff looked at Avery. "My department's done an investigation and taken pictures. We'll pass along whatever you need for your insurance. Let me know if there's anything I can do for you. I'm sorry about the loss of your house."

Following the sheriff's departure, everyone else started leaving.

"Judson." Avery knelt at the chair where he sat. He could see in her eyes that she meant to leave for a friend's house. He grabbed her hand.

"Stay."

"You're tired. You need to rest. Hodge will look in on you."

"Stay. Please."

She didn't argue. She simply rose and turned to say something to Kathy Davis in a low voice. Within minutes, the house was empty. Kathy took Brenna with her, promising to return tomorrow.

"Sleep," she said, coaxing him to a stand and wrapping her arm around his waist. He stopped them in front of the Christmas tree.

"Tomorrow's Christmas Eve."

"Yes."

He looked down at her. "Did you lose all of Brenna's gifts?"

"The ones from Santa." She closed her eyes. "Yes."

He pressed his lips to her forehead. "What about clothes?"

"I have what I took to Gabriella's apartment. And several people brought by enough to get us through a few days. I can't believe how generous everyone's been."

"You're part of the community."

After a moment, they made their way up the stairs, Ginger leading the way. In his bedroom, he sat on the side of the bed, suddenly exhausted. Avery lifted his legs on the mattress, but when she started to move away, he snagged her hand.

"Stay." He pulled and she tumbled into bed beside him.

"Judson." She managed a small laugh. "Didn't we just have this same conversation?"

"As long as it ends the same as last night." His arms wrapped around her, holding her close. "Sleep."

And he did just that.

The next morning, he awoke with Avery still beside him. As much as he desperately wanted to make love to her, he knew he needed to regain her trust.

Besides, he knew she was exhausted. Both nights, he had fuzzy memories of her placing a hand on his chest and forehead, checking to make sure he was fine, waking him just long enough to sip some cool water through a straw.

With that in mind, he eased out of bed and went downstairs. While coffee brewed, he let Ginger out. Standing on the back porch, he surveyed his ranch, picturing Avery's cabin now in smoldering ash, charred wood, broken glass, and the scattered loss of personal items. For the first time, he was grateful for their argument, because it meant she'd been somewhere else.

Going back to the kitchen, he got a few things ready. As he stepped on the bottom step to go upstairs, Avery appeared at the top.

"Good morning," he said.

"Good morning. Your voice sounds better. How do you feel?"

"A good night's sleep helped." He climbed a few steps. "I was just coming up to see if you'd like to join me for breakfast."

"Uhm, well, I should call Kathy."

"I talked with her." He took another step closer. "She'll bring Brenna over when she wakes from her afternoon nap."

"Then I'd love a cup of coffee."

"I can do better." He took her hand. "Especially since people brought over food yesterday."

She sucked in a breath when they reached the bottom of the steps. He'd turned on the Christmas tree lights and spread a blanket next to the tree. The soft sound of Christmas music played through the speakers.

"I thought we could have a Christmas Eve picnic," he said, his voice cracking, not from smoke damage but from nerves.

She sat and he poured coffee from the insulated thermos into mugs. He passed over a paper plate filled with a sausage biscuit sandwich and banana slices. When she discovered the napkins printed with candy canes, she laughed, more relaxed than he'd seen her since this whole thing started.

"I was afraid I'd never hear you laugh again."

"Judson."

"No, I don't mean the fire. I mean because of what Gaines told you."

"I shouldn't have rushed over here, primed for a fight. Especially since I didn't give you a chance to explain." She sipped her coffee. "And I didn't tell you about the phone calls."

"Will you give me a chance to explain now?" At her nod, he cleared his throat. "Gaines had one thing right—I had gone to the bank about a loan. Not a real estate loan, but a personal one. If you left for New York—not just for that first meeting about the graphic design—but if you moved there, I wanted to go with you." Her eyes went wide and she slowly lowered the mug to the floor. "The loan was to tide me over until I could find a job."

"But your ranch?"

"Remember that day you saw me coming out of Harley's office? I was there signing papers so my dad could have control of the day-to-day operations if I left."

"You would leave your father? The ranch?" She glanced around the room. "This beautiful house?"

"Avery." He reached for her hands. "None of it means anything without you. I was going to come see you today, to tell you I'd come to my senses. Well . . ." His lips curved as he kissed her knuckles. "Actually, my dad pounded some sense into me. But then I got the alert that something was wrong at your house."

"Why did you get the alert? Is it because I had my phone turned off?"

"No. I had Ed install it on my phone when he set up your system in case you needed help."

"Without telling me."

"That's right. And I'd do it again, if it meant being alerted the way I was last night." He closed his eyes. "I thought I'd lost you."

She leaned in and kissed him. "I'm right here."

"I love you, Avery." He kissed her, taking her in his arms and lowering them the floor. "Let me show you."

And to her everlasting pleasure, he did.

After he'd done everything within his power to show her how much he loved her, Judson savored the stroke of her hand up and down his back.

"You didn't give me a chance," she said.

"For what?"

"To tell you I love you back." She was smiling when he lifted his head and looked down at her. Before he could guess her intent, she rolled over and straddled him. "Now, let *me* show *you*."

SINCE THE SHERIFF had both her and Judson's cell phones—and she needed to talk with Londyn—they drove into town to buy replacements.

"Are you sure you're okay?" Londyn asked when Avery finally called her, and told her about the events of the past thirty-six hours.

"Judson's the one who was in the hospital." She sighed. "I lost the house, Londyn, and everything in it." She looked over at Judson. They still had decisions to make, but for now, all that mattered was they loved. "But they can be replaced."

When he parked in front of Kathy's house, she nodded, indicating he should go ahead. There were things she needed to tell her friend in private. "Londyn," she said, watching him walk to the front door. "I love him. And Brenna adores him. He was planning to come to New York if I moved."

"But you're not," she guessed.

"I thought about it, but only because it would mean being close to you. But I quickly realized that I want to stay here."

Even though there was food at the house from concerned neighbors, Avery wanted to stop by The Market after they picked up Brenna, and pick out something special for Christmas dinner. People stopped them, asking about Judson's condition and expressing various degrees of shock and concern over the loss of her cabin. As they roamed down an aisle Avery smiled, nudging Judson. "This brings back memories," she said as he carried Brenna and she pushed the cart.

"I have a confession to make."

"Oh?"

"I followed you here that day."

"Hoping to buy my land along with your fruit and vegetables?" she asked, failing to hold back a smile.

"I got a helluva lot more than groceries." He tickled Brenna's belly, then leaned down to kiss her. "Or land."

When they arrived back at Judson's ranch, Hodge stood next to the corral fence. "'Odge," Brenna called out before making her way through the snow to him.

"He hasn't had a cigarette in more than three weeks," Judson told her.

She leaned her head on his shoulder. "You must be proud of him."

Suddenly, Judson growled, "What the hell?" Surprised by the sharp comment, Avery straightened as Judson stormed off. Then she realized he was upset because Hodge had settled on a sled . . .with Brenna on his lap.

"Too late," Hodge called out and sent the sled down the small incline. Brenna's delighted laughter echoed through the cold sky.

For the next hour, father and son took turns giving an insistent Brenna ride after ride. Avery was hard pressed to know who was having the most fun. At one point, using the excuse of making hot chocolate, she made quick use of Judson's computer and printer before going back outside.

"Between this," she told Judson as they watched Ginger race after Hodge and Brenna on the sled. "And the short nap that Kathy said she had, Brenna will be more than ready for an early bedtime."

"Good." Judson pulled her fully into his embrace, his breath warm as his mouth skimmed hers. "We should go to bed early too, or Santa won't come. Damn," he said when she sniffed back tears. "I'm sorry, I didn't mean to remind you about losing all her presents."

"It's okay." She rested her head on his chest, watching Hodge lift Brenna onto his shoulder, just like Judson often did. "Being here, with you and Hodge, is the best gift we could have."

They did go to bed early, but it was much later before they fell asleep. Christmas morning, after texting Hodge they were awake, they came downstairs to the surprise of unexpected gifts stacked beneath the tree.

"Where did these come from?" Avery asked as Brenna ran to the tree.

"I have no idea." He crouched, looked up from reading the tag. "It says from Santa."

Tears filled her eyes—she guessed friends had somehow snuck in last night with gifts to make up for the ones they'd lost in the fire.

"Ho, Ho, Ho." Hodge came into the room.

"Horsie."

Avery cried more tears as Brenna ran over to climb onto the beautifully crafted wooden rocking horse he'd made for her.

With the floor littered in paper and boxes, and Hodge playing with Brenna, Avery offered Judson a slim box. She smiled when he tore the paper, her smile wobbling a little as he lifted the lid of the box and drew out the rolled-up slip of paper. It dropped out of his hands as he looked at her.

"You can't just do this."

"It's not official." She shrugged. "We'll have to have Harley draw up the papers."

"Avery, I don't need your land."

"You want it, you've always wanted it." She placed her hands over his. "And I want you to have it." She smiled. "Besides, since I'm basically homeless, I figured if I gave you the land, you'd let me and Brenna live here with you."

"No."

Stunned, Avery stared at him, unable to breathe, let alone say anything. He reached behind him for the lone unopened gift.

"Looks like Santa believes you've been a good girl this year."

Her heart pounding in her chest, she slowly peeled off the tape. He laughed. "Somehow I just knew you weren't the rip it open type."

"Half the fun is the anticipation."

"At this rate, it'll be the Fourth of July before you get it opened."

She rolled onto her back to stop him from snatching the gift from her. "Don't you dare."

"Hmm." He nuzzled her throat. "Maybe there's something to this idea of yours after all."

"Judson." She shoved his shoulder, pushing him back. Tears welled in her eyes when Brenna ran over to sit on his lap. Giving in, she tore off the remaining paper.

"Oh."

Inside the box, nestled on a bed of cotton, were two matching diamond bands, one much smaller than the other and suspended on a gold chain.

"I love you, Avery. I don't want to live with you." He reached for her hand, and took one of Brenna's. "I want us to be a family and make more Christmas memories. Please say you'll marry me." He cleared his throat. "I know she's too young to wear the ring yet, but, well, I thought maybe for special occasions, she could wear it as a necklace. Like the day we marry. Or, the day I adopt her." He smiled. "Maybe Harley will give us a discount."

She closed her eyes and drew in a deep breath. When she settled, just a little because this joy wasn't a feeling she wanted to take for granted in the next fifty or so years, she smiled at him. Here, under this Christmas tree was everything she could want.

"I love you, Judson, and Brenna couldn't ask for a better daddy than you."

"Daddy 'Udson."

As Judson and Avery stared at Brenna in shock, Hodge cleared his throat. "Uhm, we've been practicing."

With a watery laugh, Avery threw her arms around Judson's neck. "How in the world are we going to top this Christmas next year?"

He kissed her, then lowered his hand to her stomach. "Why don't we wish for a special Christmas delivery."

"Why don't we?"

The End

Author Biography

An award-winning author of passionate, emotional romances, Pam loves crafting stories about strong, independent women and men who discover the joy of falling in love. After years of moving as both an Army Brat and corporate wife, Pam and her craftsman husband settled in Atlanta, to be close to family and friends. Active in her local writing community, Pam also enjoys quilting, yard work, home improvement projects and spending time with her wonderful family.

You can find her at:
www.pammantovani.com.

Printed in the USA
CPSIA information can be obtained
at www.ICGtesting.com
JSHW081324221123
52184JS00009B/170